Hellfire

Alphas in Uniform Book 1

By K.L. Ramsey

Hellfire (Alphas in Uniform Book 1)
Copyright © 2020 by K.L. Ramsey.
Cover design: Michelle Sewell- RLS Images Graphics and Designs
Editing: Tracey Nyland
Imprint:Independently published

First Print Edition: March 2020
All rights reserved.

No part of this book may be reproduced, scanned, or distributed in any printed or electronic form without permission. Please do not participate in or encourage piracy of copyrighted materials in violation of the author's rights. Thank you for respecting the hard work of this author.

This is a work of fiction. Names, characters, places, and incidents either are the product of the author's imagination or are used fictitiously, and any resemblance to locales, events, business establishments, or actual persons—living or dead—is entirely coincidental.

Table of Contents

Reese	1
Dane	8
Reese	25
Dane	35
Reese	47
Dane	60
Reese	69
Dane	83
Reese	90
Dane	95
Reese	100
Dane	109
Reese	116
Dane	125
Reese	134
Dane	142
Reese	150
Dane	159
Reese	165
Dane	170
Reese	174

Dane	182
Reese	187
Dane	194
Reese	198
Dane	212
Reese	216
Dane	222
Reese	232
Dane	236

Reese

Three years earlier

Reese Summers sat at the quaint local bar which was hidden on the little stretch of beach. She was told by the hotel concierge it was a favorite hot spot and they had the best margaritas on the island. The drinks were all she really cared about since her fiancé ditched her at the altar and she was technically on her honeymoon alone. Paradise wasn't looking at all like it had in the brochures the travel agent had given them when she and David were planning their romantic getaway months before. Now, she was left explaining to just about everyone she met on the island that her fiancé got cold feet and never showed up to tie the knot. Honestly, David's feet had nothing to do with him leaving her standing in the church lobby waiting for the string quartet to play, "Here Comes the Bride"— his cock was at fault for that. Her fiancé couldn't seem to keep it out of any of her bridesmaids' vaginas and when all four of them confronted her to admit they had each slept with him, she became a stereotype. Reese ran from the church a sobbing mess in white taffeta, hailing a cab from downtown New York; wanting nothing more than to escape the embarrassment of being left at the altar. Of course, finding out the next day that David had run off with her best friend and maid of honor, Amber, felt like the final blow that had her packing her suitcase to get on the plane to head to the tropical island paradise.

Now, every moment she spent there only drove home the point that the vacation booked for two was just a painful reminder she was still a single woman and very much alone. Reese signaled the bartender that she needed another drink and sat back on her barstool. She was a fool for thinking she could run away from her problems back in New York. When she got back home tomorrow they would all still be waiting for her. Her wedding dress would still be lying on the floor of her apartment—the one she and David shared for the past two years. Her voice mail would still be full of messages from friends and family telling her how sorry they were; almost as if someone died. Her mother would be calling her to tell her she was right all along and she tried to warn Reese that David was no good for her. Her father would probably be the only person not to give her any shit but it was because he really didn't give one. Sure, she had saddled him with hundreds of thousands of dollars in bills for a wedding that never happened but what did he care—it was only money. Her father's only concern would be how to spin her being jilted at the altar in a positive light so her reputation wouldn't be tarnished at his company. Sometimes she really hated working for her father's law firm but it was easy.

When she finished law school and passed the bar, Reese wasn't sure what she wanted to do. Honestly, her first thought was to move as far away from New York as possible but her father would never allow that. He was the one who pushed her to join his firm, pointing out her last name was already in the company's logo. She hated being the boss's daughter and worried no one would ever take her seriously knowing she worked for her daddy. Reese was pretty sure being dumped at the altar would only add to the lack of respect she was already shown around the office but it wasn't something she could change. Her father had her under his thumb and until she could figure out her next move there was nothing she could do about it.

Reese was starting to feel the effects of the tequila and knowing she had a long day of travel in front of her tomorrow, she decided to call it a night and head back to her hotel. Unfortunately, the fun local bar didn't make her feel any better about her situation. If anything her fuzzy thoughts only led her down a rabbit hole of self-loathing and dread about having to return to her life. Reese was pretty sure no amount of booze was going to help her forget her problems. Though, the thought of waking up hangover free for a change sounded nice.

"Can I buy you another?" The deep baritone voice coming from behind her caught her off guard and she swiveled on her barstool to face the most gorgeous set of green eyes she had ever seen. He smiled down at her and she almost felt like laughing in the poor guy's face. His brown hair was slicked back as if he had just come from a swim in the ocean and his beard made her wonder if the rumors were true. David was always clean-shaven, but some of her friends' husbands had joined the new beard fad and they like to boast about how the stubble tickled—all over.

"Listen, you look like a nice guy but I'm not in the mood for small talk. The last thing I want to do is get to know you and I'm betting you will feel the same way about me in about five seconds." Reese knew she sounded like a bitch but there was no helping it.

"Why five seconds?" he asked.

"Because it's all the time it will take for me to tell you I'm here on my honeymoon—alone." Reese turned back to the bar certain her would-be suitor had already high tailed it out of there. Hell, he had plenty of other prospects to keep him company. The bar was packed tonight; not that she wanted or needed anyone else's company. She just wanted to have a few drinks and wallow in her self-pity.

"I'm sorry to hear your ex-fiancé is a fucking loser," he said, still behind her. Reese turned to face him again and plastered on her best smile. It must not have been too convincing judging by the way he laughed at her. She wasn't used to anyone laughing at her and honestly she wasn't a fan.

"Are you hard- up—um, I didn't catch your name," she admitted.

"That's because I didn't throw it," he said. "It's Dane, by the way. I'm a lifeguard on the island." Reese rolled her eyes and tried to turn back around. She had heard a lot of bad pick-up lines in her life but this guy seemed to be the king of cheesy. She wondered if his whole lifeguard routine usually worked on women. Dane put his hand on her chair, effectively stopping her from being able to turn away from him.

"Sorry honey but I think you must have misunderstood me. I just want to buy you a drink." Reese's laugh sounded mean, even to her own ears.

"My name isn't honey and I told you I'm good," she spat. "If you want to offer me something—" Reese paused, looking him up and down. She wasn't sure why she even said the next part, but the words were out of her mouth before she even knew what she was doing. "You can take me back to my hotel room and fuck me until I forget your bad pick-up line, Dane." Reese noticed how his eyes flared and she was pretty sure he was going to take her up on her offer. Hell, she was basically giving him a night of strings free sex. What red-blooded man would refuse such an offer?

"Fine," he agreed. Dane helped her down from the barstool and handed her bag to her. "Where are you staying, honey?" he asked.

"Reese," she offered. She wasn't quite sure what she had just agreed to, but from the look of him, Dane would be able to help her forget about David, at least for one night. And honestly, she would be grateful for the reprieve. She wanted to fuck—that was it and hopefully, forget all the feelings that plagued her every day for the past week.

"Sorry?" he said.

"My name—it's Reese." She took his offered hand and let him lead her out of the crowd and through the open double doors leading to the deck outside. It was suddenly way too quiet for her and she worried about what she had just done. She agreed to go back to her hotel room with a complete stranger. Wasn't this how women ended up on the news? Reese knew better than to do something so foolish but she honestly didn't care.

"It's good to meet you, Reese," Dane held his hand out and she shook it. With the formalities out of the way, she wasn't sure just what to do next.

"Are you sure you are up for this?" he asked. Reese nodded her head, not wanting to back down now. She wanted this—one night of pleasure, just for herself.

"I'm sure," she stuttered. "Can you give me that, Dane? I just want to forget everything about this last week." Reese didn't miss the pity in his eyes as he looked her up and down. Sure, she saw the desire when his eyes landed on her ample chest. Most guys looked at her that way and she had grown used to it, but Dane seemed to see through her tough girl exterior and could tell she wasn't all she was pretending to be.

"I think I can handle you, honey," he promised. He once again held out his hand and Reese didn't hesitate to take it. She was going to do this for herself and then she could head back to New York and clean up the mess David left for her because it was who she was—like it or not.

K.L. Ramsey

Dane

Dane Knight wasn't sure just what to do about sexy little Reese. Well, he knew what he wanted to do to her but he had never met anyone with such sad eyes before. They were the prettiest hazel eyes he had ever seen, so big and trusting but filled with so much pain. He wanted to pull her against his body and tell her she was going to be alright but he didn't know her. Hell, if she spent the night with him she probably wouldn't be alright. He had a way of fucking up everyone's life and he worried the pretty little brunette was just going to end up as collateral damage.

He was never one to turn down a good time, but a part of him wished she would have told him no; not that he wouldn't have pushed her to change her mind. He usually broke the ice by offering to buy a pretty woman a drink. He liked to hook up with women who were there on vacation. Dane didn't like relationships and things tended to get messy when he dated local girls. They seemed to hang around and expect him to be boyfriend material and he wasn't. He was more of a one night stand kind of guy and most women he took to bed knew the score. Dane was out for a good time, some easy fun and that was about it. He worried he was in over his head with feisty little Reese. When she admitted she was on her honeymoon alone it just about broke his damn heart. He should have walked away from her right then and there but he couldn't. Apparently, his dick was in charge and his cock wanted Reese. He couldn't blame his dick for wanting her either; she was easy on the eyes with those sultry, pouty lips. He was hard just from thinking about what he wanted to do with her.

Reese was staying on the north end of the island in a little bungalow right on the beach. Apparently, she was staying in the honeymoon suite and Dane wondered if they couldn't switch her room for her or if pretty Reese was a masochist.

"This is me," she whispered shyly. Dane noticed the same woman who blatantly asked him for sex was nowhere to be found. Instead, Reese turned into a shy, timid woman who seemed completely unsure of what she wanted.

"It's alright if you've changed your mind, honey," Dane offered.

"No!" she shouted, shaking her head. "Please, don't leave. I'm sure I want this. It's just not something I usually do. I don't pick up strangers in bars and ask them for sex. I've never been with anyone besides my fiancée," Reese admitted. She laughed, "Although he couldn't say the same. Apparently, he had no trouble asking women for sex, starting with my entire bridal party."

Dane winced. "That's rough, Reese. I'm sorry for what he did to you, but maybe you are better off not being married to him. Trust me; I don't think his extracurricular activities would have ended with a legally binding piece of paper." Dane shuddered at the thought of having something like that with a woman. He hadn't met one he wanted to spend the rest of his life with and he was pretty sure that fact would never change.

"Yeah, I dodged a real bullet." She laughed. "Listen, I know what I'm doing here, Dane and I'd like for you to spend the night with me if you want to." Reese looked up at him and hell; he knew he'd be game for just about anything she wanted. He just hoped he wasn't making a giant mistake. He usually picked up women who were on vacation, just out to have a good time. He had a feeling Reese wasn't necessarily looking for a good time as much as she was searching for a way to forget her pain, even for just one night. He could give her that at least.

"I'd like that, thank you," Dane said. He crossed the room and pulled open the minibar. "Drink?" he asked.

"Sure," she said, giggling. "My ex is paying for this vacation, so why the hell not?" Dane pulled out a few miniatures of booze and a soda to make them both a drink.

He mixed two rum and cokes and handed one to Reese. "Thanks," she said. She chugged it down like a sorority girl at a frat party. "Another?" she squeaked. He smiled at her and took her cup. Dane worried if he plied her with too much more alcohol she wouldn't be coherent enough to remember her own name, let alone his.

"Please," she asked when he made no move to get her another drink. Dane crossed to the minibar and made her another drink, careful not to add as much rum to this one and handed it to her. Reese seemed none the wiser and chugged it down too.

He decided to get the party started, not wanting to give her a chance to ask him for another drink. Dane pulled his shirt off and liked Reese's reaction at seeing him half-naked. She seemed to need to touch him, tracing his full tattoo sleeve up his arm and over his chest. Goosebumps rose on his skin and he reached for her, pulling her into his arms.

"Who's Cole?" she asked, kissing her way up his shoulder.

"Hm?" he murmured. Dane was having trouble focusing on her words; her hands and mouth felt so fucking good.

"Cole?" Reese stopped kissing his arm and pointed to the name he had displayed on his bicep. Most women didn't pay enough attention to him to see what was written inside the intricate tattoo that banded its way up from his wrist to his shoulder. They usually cared more about what he was going to do to them rather than notice any personal details about him.

"Cole was my father's name," he whispered. "It was my first tat. I got it after my dad died and added everything else later," he said. He really didn't like talking about his father. In fact, he hated it.

"I'm sorry," Reese said. "How old were you when he died?" she asked.

"Fifteen." His voice gave him away and he knew if he didn't change the course of their conversation he'd end up using her as a psychiatrist and not for sex. That wasn't what tonight was supposed to be about. He promised Reese a night of sex, no strings attached and talking about his father felt like a fucking string.

"You have on too many clothes, honey," he whispered, changing the topic. Reese smiled up at him seeming to be alright with not talking anymore. He breathed out his relief and watched as she grabbed the hem of her shirt to tug it up over her head.

"Well, how about we do something to remedy the situation, Dane?" She pulled her shirt up and over her head, tossing it to the floor. She wasn't wearing a bra and the sight of her bare breasts had his mouth-watering.

"You're beautiful, Reese," he insisted. She shyly looked down at the floor but Dane wouldn't let her hide from him. He hooked a finger under her chin forcing her to look at him. "No hiding," he whispered. She smiled up at him as if accepting his challenge.

"It's just been a damn long time since anyone has said those words to me," she said. Her admission made his heart stutter and Dane quickly shut it down. There was no room for feelings in what he wanted from sexy little Reese. He pushed her auburn hair back from her face and dragged her up his body to kiss his way into her mouth. She willingly let his tongue gain entry and he stroked his way in loving the breathy little sighs and moans he elicited from her. She was so willing, so sweet and he was pretty sure he'd find her wet and ready for whatever he wanted to do with her.

Reese wrapped her arms around Dane's neck and he took it as his cue she was all in. He lifted her into his arms, letting her legs straddle his waist and walked them back to the big bed which sat in the middle of the room. Dane dug his fingers into her ass through her skimpy cut-off shorts, loving the way she filled his hands.

"Yes, Reese hissed into his mouth. "I need more, please Dane." He wouldn't let her beg him for long. She was driving him completely crazy and he felt a raw need to consume her, taste her, mark her and make her his. Dane nipped and sucked his way down her body helping her to shimmy out of her skimpy little shorts. He looked up her curvy body to find Reese watching him, biting her lip as if in anticipation of what he was about to do to her. Dane sent her a wolfish grin and settled between her legs, parting her wet folds to lick his way into her pussy.

"Mmm," he moaned against her slick core. She shivered and groaned at the sensation. Reese shamelessly ground her pussy against his mouth and he loved how she so brazenly took what she wanted from him.

"I'm so close," she shouted, running her hands through his hair and tugging the ends. She wasn't gentle and her all-consuming need turned him completely on. It had been some time since Dane had been with a woman who gave as good as she got and Reese didn't disappoint in that area. She was a vixen and he loved the way she demanded more from him. Dane slid two fingers into her core and pumped them in and out of her slick opening, sucking her clit into his mouth until she nearly bucked off the bed. He pressed her against the mattress with his shoulders not allowing her to move, forcing her to take every ounce of pleasure he was giving her.

After Reese's second orgasm, he couldn't wait anymore; he needed to be inside of her. She laid across the bed wrung out from the pleasure he'd given her and Dane felt his inner caveman thump his chest. He didn't give her any warning; didn't ask if she was ready for him. He wanted to just take what he needed from her the same way Reese had taken what she wanted from him.

Dane unbuttoned his shorts and let them fall to the floor. He sunk into her body, snugly fitting into her until he was balls deep. They both moaned at the pleasure of it all. "You feel so fucking good, Reese," he moaned. She gifted him with her sexy smile and reached for his body. Dane covered her with his own and pressed her into the mattress.

"You feel good too, Dane," she whispered against his lips. He pumped in and out of her body taking everything she was willing to give him and pushing her for more.

"Fuck, honey," he growled. "I'm going to come." Dane found his release and collapsed on top of Reese. "Thank you, honey," he whispered against her neck. Reese wrapped her arms and legs around him pulling him tighter against her body.

"That was so good," she murmured. He could tell she was already drifting off probably due to the alcohol and the orgasms he had just given to her. "I love you, David," she whispered around a yawn.

"David," he questioned. "Who the fuck is David?" He pushed up from the bed and Reese's arms and legs easily let him go. Dane realized she was sound asleep. A part of him wanted to wake her the fuck up and ask her to explain, but the asshole side of him saw this as his way to slip quietly from her room. It was what he usually did; why should tonight be any different? Maybe it was the way she called him by another man's name. It hurt. It shouldn't have but it did. He was so careful not to call a woman by her name usually opting for calling her honey. It was the hazard of picking up women at bars and never seeing them again after their one night together. But Reese demanded he not call her honey and now she went and called him by some other guy's name.

Dane covered Reese with a blanket and noted her sexy curves as she curled up on her side to cuddle into the pillow which laid next to her body. He pulled on his shorts and t-shirt, finding his shoes by the door where he left them and slipped out of her bungalow. The walk of shame usually didn't bother him but tonight for some reason it did. Maybe it was the way Reese seemed to desperately need him or maybe it was the way she told him she loved him just before she fell asleep. Dane needed to remember she wasn't really talking to him. Reese was telling some other fucker named David that she was in love with him and it really pissed Dane off. He'd never heard those words before, well—unless he counted his mother telling him she loved him. Maybe it was what threw him off his game. He needed to remember what Reese Summers was to him—just a hook-up no matter how her words seemed to fill his head or his heart, she wasn't his.

―――――――――

Present Day

Dane heard the doorbell and he yelled for Jace to grab the door, rolling over to try to catch a few more minutes of sleep. When it rang twice more Dane remembered he was minus one roommate since his friend moved out to live with his new wife. He wanted to be grumpy about the fact he was left high and dry and the way Jace broke bro code, falling for a woman and dumping him, but he was also thrilled for his friend. The doorbell sounded again and he grumbled about not being given even a moment's peace.

He got out of bed pulling on a pair of gym shorts and stumbled his way to the door. "This better be pretty fucking important," he growled, throwing the door open. A pretty little brunette stood on the other side of the threshold holding a little boy in her arms.

"Hi, Dane," she whispered. He looked her up and down noting she looked familiar, but he knew many women. This woman wasn't one he could easily forget though. Unlike the other women Dane hooked up with; she haunted him for months after their one night together.

"Sorry, do I know you?" he asked, keeping up the facade. The woman seemed put off by the fact he didn't know who she was and little alarms were sounding in his brain. The only reason she would be upset about him not knowing her would be if he slept with her and forgot. He slept with a lot of women and she wasn't the first to show up on his doorstep pissed she wasn't the most important woman from his past.

The little guy in her arms squirmed and twisted trying to get down. "Stay still, please," she scolded, startling the toddler.

"Go," he cried but she readjusted her hold and stared Dane down.

"You seriously don't remember me, Dane? Three years ago-rundown bar on the beach, jilted bride. My name is Reese. Is any of this ringing a bell?" She seemed to be getting angrier by the minute and honestly, he did remember her. Dane sometimes saw her hazel eyes in his dreams. He hated admitting he knew her but he did. He remembered her story about being left at the altar by some asshole who couldn't keep his dick in his pants. Dane remembered the way she looked at him with her sad lost eyes and how he wished he could be what she needed but he couldn't. He remembered everything about the night they shared together, but he wouldn't admit it to Reese.

"So, what brings you to my doorstep?" he asked. He wouldn't admit to knowing her now, it would be easier to send her on her way if he kept up the pretense that he didn't recognize her. And that was exactly what he planned on doing; sending sexy little Reese and the kid squirming in her arms as far away as possible. The last time he saw her he spent almost a year trying to forget her.

"He brings me to your doorstep, Dane," she sassed, motioning to the squirming toddler. He smiled at the little boy and waved.

"He seems a little young to be driving, don't you think?" Dane teased. Reese sighed and held the child out towards him letting him dangle in midair.

"Take a good long look, smart ass. He's got your eyes and I'm guessing he also inherited your crappy disposition since I'm not half as moody as our kid." Dane looked the little boy over and swore. He couldn't deny the little guy had his eyes but that proved nothing. He was sure there were millions of guys in the world with brown hair and green eyes who could claim to be the kid's father.

"Our matching eye color and moodiness is hardly proof I'm his father," Dane denied.

"Listen, I'm willing to submit to a DNA test if it will make you happy, but we're here because we need help," Reese pulled the toddler back against her body and wrapped her arms around him.

"I see," Dane sighed. She was there to shake him down for money. It wasn't the first time he had a woman show up on his doorstep trying to sell him a sad story that ended with her asking him for cash. "How much do you two need, honey?" he asked.

Reese's expression went from mildly upset to completely pissed and if Dane wasn't mistaken, hurt. "I don't need money," she spat. "I have plenty of money and if you spent more than five minutes trying to get to know me, you would have known that about me, Dane."

Maybe he had misread the situation but she wanted something. Why would she show up now with a kid in tow claiming to need his help? "Alright, so you don't need money. What is it you need?"

Reese readjusted the squirming toddler on her hip. "You know, you haven't even asked his name." She eyed him suspiciously and he shrugged.

"Does it matter? I don't believe he's mine so why do I need to know his name?" Dane knew he sounded like a cold-hearted bastard but he didn't care. He had an early shift at the fire station in the morning and he wanted to get back to his bed.

"His name is Cole," she whispered.

"That was my father's name," Dane said. Why would some chick he spent a few hours with name her kid after his father? Alarms were sounding in his head again, but he didn't want to believe her story could be true. He looked the boy over once more and noticed the subtle similarities between the two of them. The kid had the same dimple in his chin as Dane did and if he wasn't mistaken he looked a hell of a lot like his baby pictures his mother liked to drag out when he made the trip back home. If Reese was telling the truth and the kid was his why did it take her three fucking years to tell him?

"Okay, let's say the kid is mine," he whispered. "Why the hell are you telling me now? Didn't I have a right to know when he was born maybe or how about when you found out you were pregnant with my kid?"

Reese seemed to put up her defenses at his question. She defiantly raised her chin, "I didn't think you'd care. I was a one night stand, Dane. Hell, you could barely remember my name. How was I to believe you'd want to have any part in Cole's life?" Hearing his father's name again did strange things to his heart. His father would have never turned away a kid, his or not. But Dane wasn't his father. He would never measure up to be half the man his dad was and he was reminded of that fact every time he reported to duty down at the fire station. His dad's plaques and pictures hung in memoriam for saving a family's four small kids who were trapped in their burning house. Dane heard time and again how thankful they were to his dad. He saved another family the pain of being torn apart while he and his mother had to learn to live with the devastation of losing him. Their family had been changed forever, but Dane had the consolation of knowing his old man died a hero.

"I know this is a lot for you to take in and maybe I misjudged you—maybe I should have told you about him, but we are here now and we are in trouble." Reese's voice cracked and for the first time since Dane answered the door, he saw just how afraid she was.

"Tell me what you need," he whispered. He knew if he turned her away now he might never see either of them again and he wasn't really sure how he felt about the whole having a kid thing.

"I think someone is trying to hurt Cole and I'm not sure who or why," she said. "I received this letter at work last week." She reached into her jacket pocket and pulled out a crumpled piece of paper.

"You won't win, bitch." Dane read the note aloud. "We will make sure you pay one way or another starting with that adorable kid of yours," he finished. Dane studied the letter noting whoever sent it at least took the time to type it up. He expected a letter like that to be spelled out in block letters cut from a magazine and glued to the paper. He folded the note and handed it back to her. Reese took it, shoving it back into her pocket.

"I can't lose him," she sobbed. Reese broke down and Dane wasn't sure just what to do. Her whole body shook with her sobs and a part of him wanted to give her privacy. He never knew what to do with a crying woman and Reese was no exception. Dane sighed and closed the distance between the two of them, hesitantly wrapping her and Cole in his arms. The toddler squirmed between the two of them and Dane took him from Reese.

"Sit," he told her. She surprisingly did as he ordered and he shut his front door.

"Sorry," she said. Reese smiled up to where he stood holding Cole and even managed a giggle.

Dane would never understand women. One minute they were crying, the next laughing hysterically. He and Cole just looked at Reese as if she had lost her mind. He really didn't know her and hell, maybe she was always a lunatic.

"Wanna share what's so funny?" he asked. Reese pointed up at him and Cole.

"You two," she gasped. "I thought Cole looked like you before. But now with you holding him, it's like seeing double." Reese fell back against his sofa holding her stomach, laughing. He looked Cole over and wasn't sure if he found the whole situation as funny as Reese did. Of course, he had about two years of catching up to do to get to the point she was at.

"Reese," he grumbled, "Are we going to figure this out or not? Do you want my help?" Reese seemed to sober at the mention of him helping her and Cole.

"Yes," she said. "I don't just want your help, I need it. I think our son's life depends on it." Dane hoped she was just being overly dramatic, but there was no way he'd turn the two of them away, no matter how badly he wanted to just crawl back into his bed and pretend her visit was all just a bad dream.

"Fine," Dane agreed. "I'll help you but I'm going to want some answers. In the meantime, you can both stay here. My roommate just moved out and you can take his room until we can figure this all out." Dane really didn't like the idea of having his one-night-stand staying in the next room along with a kid who may or may not be his.

Reese nodded, "Thank you," she said. Dane looked her up and down not knowing where to even start. This was uncharted territory for him, but he had a feeling he was going to have to learn to sink or swim fast. What other choice did he have?

Reese

Reese wasn't sure what to do or say next and the way Dane was eyeing her screaming toddler she worried he was going to change his mind and rescind his offer to let them stay with him. She'd be the first to admit she wouldn't blame him—Cole was a handful; he always had been.

"He'll stop fussing," she promised. "He's just really tired; we both are. I've been driving around in circles for days now trying to figure out my next move," she admitted.

"Well, I can show you to your room and you can put him to bed," Dane offered. Reese nodded and followed him as he led the way back to his spare room.

"I really appreciate you doing this, Dane," she yelled over Cole's continued screeches. Dane shrugged as if it wasn't a big deal, but she noticed the way his shoulders bunched every time her son cried out as if he was being physically harmed.

"He's a pretty dramatic little guy," Dane laughed as Cole arched his back wanting to be put down.

Reese found her son's theatrics less funny than his father did but it might be because she was privy to them for the past two years and this was all brand new for Dane. "Yeah," she said dryly. "He's a little actor, alright. Let me get him changed and settled and then I'll answer all of your questions." Dane hesitated and she realized it was late for him too. "That is unless you'd like for me to wait until morning," she offered.

"No, I think we need to get a few things cleared up before morning," Dane said looking her and Cole over. "If you are going to be here for a while we'll probably need some ground rules, too." Reese cringed at the mention of rules. She had enough of those growing up in her father's house. She hated the idea of her own child having to abide by his father's strict rules and consequential punishments.

"Maybe this was a bad idea," she whispered. "I can find someplace else to stay as soon as I can find a job, but I won't have you implementing strict rules that are completely unfair to my son. He's just a toddler and doesn't understand right from wrong yet." She picked Cole back up from where she had laid him on the big bed. He had quieted down and wasn't happy about being disturbed.

Dane chuckled, "I think you misunderstood, honey. I really don't have any rules for the kid. Hell, I think he should be able to do whatever it is most two-year-olds do. I meant ground rules for you and me," he said pointing between the two of them.

"Rules for you and me?" she asked.

"Yep," he answered. "Things like—don't go getting any ideas about wanting a relationship with me. Oh, and don't expect me to be home every night. I'm out most nights and don't come home until the early morning hours usually. I'll try to be quiet of course but I can't make any promises." Dane smiled and she could feel her cheeks heat. He was basically telling her he didn't want to get involved with her and not to expect him to stay home with her and Cole. The way he boasted about staying out most nights until morning was her favorite part though. It really drove home the fact that in almost three years Dane hadn't changed one bit. Although, she really hadn't expected him to suddenly be settled down and more mature, on some level she hoped he would be—at least for her son's sake.

"Don't worry, Dane," she groused. "I'm pretty sure I remember the score. You did leave me passed out in my hotel room after you finished using me," she said. His expression seemed to sour at the mention of their night together and she worried she had gone too far. He was kind enough to take her and Cole in even if he made her feel like they were unwanted intruders in his life and she was grateful for the place to stay.

"Listen." Reese sighed, "I don't want to cramp your style. We will stay out of your way as much as humanly possible and I'll find us another place to stay just as soon as I can get some cash together. I can't use my credit cards in case they are tracking me," she whispered. Reese laid Cole back down onto the bed since he had fallen asleep on her shoulder and held her finger to her lips, signaling for Dane to be quiet. Reese watched as he studied Cole and then followed her out of the room. She knew meeting his son had to be a lot for him to take in, but Reese had to admit he was taking it well.

Dane led the way to his kitchen and pulled two beers from the fridge, handing her one. "Thanks," she whispered.

"I know it's not tequila, but I figure last time you drank the hard stuff around me we made a kid so maybe we just stick with beer," Dane teased. At least, Reese thought he was teasing but she had no point of reference to go from.

"I know me just showing up on your doorstep and dumping all of this on you is a lot to take in, Dane. I'm sorry. Believe me, if I had any other choice I wouldn't be here now but I'm desperate to keep Cole safe." Dane nodded and took a long swig of his beer.

"So, if your lives weren't in danger I would have never found out I have a son? You would have just continued on with your daily existence and what, Cole would have grown up never knowing me?" Reese felt bad but she wouldn't lie to him. He was correct she would have never told him about Cole and she would have tried to be enough for their son. Lots of kids grew up without fathers. Hell, she would have probably been better off if that had been the case for her. Instead, she grew up with an overbearing controlling ass for a father and if her hunch was correct he was behind the plot to hurt her and Cole.

She nodded, "I know it all makes me sound like a stone-cold bitch but as I said earlier, I was just a one night stand. Why would I show up here pregnant to tell you that you were going to be a father? Would you have even cared, Dane? Her question sounded more like an accusation, but judging from the way Dane mean mugged her, she had made the correct assumption.

"Fuck," he spat, pacing his little kitchen. "I have no idea how I would have reacted to the news you were pregnant with my baby but I'll never know now, will I? You took that away from me, honey." Reese hated the way he so easily turned the tables on her. She was a good lawyer and she hated losing an argument but Dane had a damn good point. She had taken his choice away from him and it was a regret she would have to live with.

When she had found out she was pregnant months after her one night with Dane, she worried the baby might be David's. But a quick paternity test after Cole was born had proven otherwise. David showed up at the hospital to submit his sample and told her no matter what the results were, he wanted nothing to do with the baby. He explained he had no time for a kid and it would ruin his professional plans. She wanted to laugh at the whole scenario—what about her professional plans? She was relieved when the results came back he wasn't the father. Reese thought about letting Dane know about the baby, but she also remembered how he left her that night after their brief encounter. He made her feel so cheap and used she wasn't sure she wanted to have any contact with Dane again. She sure as hell didn't want him to make her son feel unwanted, so she opted to not tell him. As far as she was concerned Dane could remain blissfully ignorant about the baby they created and she would learn to be everything their son would need, rolled up in a one-parent package.

"I'm sorry Dane—you're right. I did take away your choice and you have every right to be pissed off at me for it. I messed up and thought I was making the best decision for Cole. If I had known you might have wanted a relationship with him, I would have done things differently," she admitted.

Is there any chance he isn't my son?" Dane asked.

Reese stared down at the floor not wanting to admit this next part. "At first, I thought he might be David's," she said.

"David?" Dane asked.

"Yeah," Reese hated that she was going to have to repeat her sordid past, but why would Dane remember her sad story of being left at the altar? Heck, he didn't even remember her name. "David was the man who left me at the altar and the reason I was on this island by myself. I used our honeymoon trip to escape reality."

Dane nodded, "I think I remember some of it, honey." Reese rolled her eyes at him.

"Reese, my name is Reese, not honey," she corrected. Dane chuckled at her and she didn't hide her smile. She remembered him to be a charmer, but she forgot just how good looking he was with his dark brown hair and soulful green eyes. Dane still had facial hair and she had to admit she liked it. Reese found his whole look quite sexy but it wasn't why she was here. She needed to remember no good would come from her falling for him and she was only staying in his condo to save her little boy.

"Now that I remember, honey," Dane confirmed. "You thought I didn't know your name but I did. I still do. Hell Reese, I spent the better part of a year trying to forget your name," he whispered. Dane took a step towards her and she couldn't help but lean into his big body. It had been so long since any man had touched her; almost three years to be exact. Dane Knight was the last man she had been with, but admitting the truth to him wasn't an option.

"How did you find me, Reese?" he asked, changing the subject.

She welcomed the topic change, needing to put a little emotional distance between them. But, she had to wonder just what he meant by him needing to take a year to forget her name. That would be a question she saved for another time, preferably one when her overly active hormones weren't ruling her body.

"Well, it is a long story," she said. "After the paternity test proved David wasn't Cole's father, the only other man I had been with was you. I toyed with the notion of telling you, but had no idea who you were so I hired a private detective to dig up some information on you." She sheepishly shrugged at him knowing how it all sounded.

"Shit," he cursed. You had a PI digging around my personal life, looking me up?" Sure, when he said it like that it sounded bad.

"You have to understand, Dane. I was a new mother with no emotional support or help and I wasn't going to just let a complete stranger into my or my son's life," she said. She knew she sounded defensive and had no real right to be but she would do the same thing all over again. One thing she learned from her father was you can't trust anyone, not even family.

"I'm not a stranger. I'm his father," Dane shouted, pointing down the hallway to where Cole slept.

"I get it, I really do. But, at the time I had to protect both him and me. I didn't even know your last name, Dane. All I knew about you was your first name and you said that you were a lifeguard. What was I supposed to do? Show up on the island and just start shouting your name and hope you might pop up to answer?"

"Now you're just being downright ridiculous," Dane accused. He pointed his finger at her and Reese stifled her giggle. She felt almost as if he was scolding a small child and it made her think of Cole. They looked so much alike; they even had some of the same facial expressions, especially when they were angry.

"It's not funny, Reese," he grouched.

She tried to sober, really she did. But the angrier he got the more Dane reminded her of her son. Reese giggled, "Sorry, but you remind me of Cole when he has a tantrum," she admitted. Reese covered her mouth with her hand hiding her smile.

"I can't do this with you laughing at me," Dane complained.

"Fine, I'm sorry," she said. "I will try not to make comparisons that might strike me as humorous. And you're right, Dane. I should have tried harder to find you on my own. I screwed up and I'm sorry. I really thought I was doing what was best for Cole," she said.

"So, I'm not good enough to be a father to my son?" he questioned. Reese had a feeling no matter what she said or how she worded things, Dane was going to find fault with her. He was angry and she couldn't blame him.

"I think we could both use a time out," she said. "How about we get some sleep and then pick this up tomorrow?" she asked.

Dane nodded, "Alright," he conceded. "Tomorrow. We're going to have a nice long talk about who exactly is after you and what they might want. I have a few connections down at the local police department who might be able to give us a hand," he said.

"Thank you, Dane—for everything," she whispered. Reese took a chance he wouldn't think she was coming on to him and went up on her tiptoes to gently kiss Dane's cheek. He had a deer in the headlights stare and she couldn't help her giggle. "It's just a thank you, Dane. Don't read too much into it." She headed back down the hall to where Cole was still sound asleep and quietly shut her bedroom door, leaving Dane standing in the kitchen. She wasn't sure if she could count their whole conversation as a success but it had gone better than she could have hoped. She had practice talks in her head the whole drive to Dane's place and none of them went as well as their actual chat had. All in all, she'd count tonight as a win and just hoped tomorrow's conversation would go half as well.

Hellfire

Dane

Dane woke to the sound of shrieking giggles that reminded him of his childhood. He rolled over in his bed and checked the time, groaning when he realized it was just past six in the morning. His alarm wasn't set to go off for another hour and after his late-night conversation with Reese, he could have used an extra hour of sleep.

Cole's giggle floated down the hall and he smiled thinking about mornings with his own dad and the way he used to tickle him to get him to giggle like that. Dane wondered how his dad would have felt about being a grandpa. Hell, he was going to have to eventually tell his mother he fucked up and got a woman pregnant but he was pretty sure his mother was going to be thrilled. She had made him her personal project and called Dane every couple days to remind him neither of them was getting any younger and a grandchild would give her life fulfillment. He usually laughed or grumbled something about her minding her own business but this time he'd have something new to tell her. He just wondered how long it would take his mother to show up on his doorstep ready to take over grandmother duty. Dane made a mental note to warn Reese about his mother before he gave his mom the news about Cole. It might be safer for all involved if his mother came with a warning label, but maybe that was just his opinion.

Dane wondered what Reese meant when she said she was a new mother with no emotional support. Did she not have any family or friends that could help her or was she truly alone? That thought made him sad. Dane had his mom and a few good friends. He wasn't sure what he would do without them and the support they all gave to each other. Hell, he wouldn't have followed his dream and became a firefighter if it wasn't for his best friends Jace and Nico pushing him to do it.

He was about to get out of bed and hit the shower when his bedroom door flew open and Cole came bursting into his room. "Hi," the toddler yelled and jumped onto his bed. He started to sing a song Dane wasn't familiar with while bouncing around. He didn't even stop when Reese came running in after him scolding him to sit down and cut it out.

"No," Cole shouted and continued to jump around Dane. He wanted to get up or at least move out of the kid's way, but he was sporting a pretty impressive morning wood and worried about getting out of bed in just his boxer briefs. Instead, he rolled to the side and groaned.

"I'm so sorry, Dane," Reese offered. If his cock wasn't so hard he'd find the whole thing funny. But he was in the middle of a pretty major dry spell and his morning routine usually consisted of him getting off in the shower to start his day. His new job left little time for trolling the local bars for women to fill his nights with. Besides, he was exhausted by the whole scene, but he wouldn't tell Reese that, especially not with the way he went on about her and Cole not cramping his style last night. Hell, he hadn't shared his lack of sex life with anyone including his friends. He wasn't in the mood to hear how proud they were of him for turning over a new leaf. His friend Jace had been riding his ass for months now trying to get him to have a meaningful relationship with a woman—whatever that meant. Dane had really never dated and as for relationships, he didn't do them. They tended to get a little messy and he liked easy. Fat lot of good easy hook-ups turned out to be, especially judging from the fact his current little houseguest was a product of one of the hottest one night stands he ever had.

Dane looked Reese up and down realizing she was only wearing a skimpy t-shirt and panties and she must have noticed his stare. She tried to pull the shirt down her body but it didn't help; only exposing her perfect breasts to him. He smiled up at her and she smirked.

"Well, it's not as if you haven't seen it all already," she teased, giving up the fight to hide her body. Dane chuckled. She was right and he wouldn't mind seeing it all again, although he'd never admit that to her.

"Since we are taking stances, honey—" Dane stood up from the bed, his impressive erection tented his boxer briefs and immediately caught her stare and Reese made no move to look away or pretend she hadn't seen it. "I have to pee and take a shower. It's not like you've never seen it before, honey," he said, throwing her words back at her. Dane smiled over to Reese as she tried to corral Cole from jumping on his bed.

"Is it okay if I make him some breakfast? I'll pay you back for any food we use," she said.

"Sure, help yourself," Dane offered, heading into his bathroom. "Don't worry about paying me back, it's not a big deal," he shouted through the door. He listened for Reese to convince Cole to go with her for some food and started up the shower. He'd get his unruly cock under control and then he'd hopefully have a few minutes to sit down and talk to Reese. They needed to finish their discussion from last night and he wanted to get a handle on exactly who was after her and why they would go after Cole. The sooner he could help Reese the sooner he could get his life back in order.

Dane found Reese and Cole sitting at his kitchen table eating pancakes and bananas and the sight stopped him cold. Reese was making airplane sounds trying to coax the toddler to eat the bananas instead of double-fisting the pancakes. Dane had to admit the kid had the right idea. He'd pick pancakes over fruit any day of the week.

Reese looked up from feeding Cole and it sounded like her airplane took a nosedive. He couldn't help his chuckle and she smiled sheepishly back at him. "I hope this is okay." She motioned to the mess around the kitchen and he shrugged. He was used to messes since Jace wasn't the neatest roommate, but Dane was more of a neat freak. Still, he could roll with the punches and having Reese and Cole in his space might not be ideal but it was necessary.

"It's fine, Reese," he said. He made his way to the coffee pot and poured himself a cup. He had a feeling he was going to need a few cups to get through the day ahead. "I have to head into work," he said. Honestly, he felt like he was giving her an apology and maybe he was. "I hate having to leave the two of you here to fend for yourselves, but I can't switch my shift on such short notice."

"No, I wouldn't expect you to change your work schedule for us. I'm the one interrupting your life. You do what you have to do, Dane. I just didn't think the beaches would be open this early in the spring," Reese said.

"Beaches?" he asked. Dane wondered if she was planning on a day trip to the beach. Honestly, if she was in as much danger as he thought, she and the kid should just hang in his condo.

"Yeah, when we met you said you were a lifeguard. If I remember correctly, it was your go-to pick-up line that night." Reese shrugged and shoved a piece of banana into Cole's mouth only to have it spat back into her hand. Dane laughed and Reese shot him a look telling him she found the whole scene less funny than he did.

"Really Dane, you are going to have to find our son a lot less funny," she chastised. "He will never learn to behave if we laugh at every adorable thing this kid does." Dane gave her a curt nod but didn't make her any promises.

"Well, I'm a firefighter now," he offered. "I quit lifeguarding months back and went through the training."

"Wow," Reese said. "That's wonderful, Dane. What made you choose firefighting?" she asked. Dane wasn't sure a woman had ever asked him about his personal life—well, except his mother. An actual conversation with a woman was new to him. Sure his friends' women, Toni and Heather, asked questions and seemed to care about him but he had never had sex with either of them. It was kind of nice the way Reese seemed to take an interest in him.

"Nevermind," Reese whispered, "I shouldn't pry into your private life," she said. Dane hated that he hesitated and made Reese feel as though she had done something wrong.

"No, it's fine," he said. Dane sat down at the table across from Reese and she handed him a plate of pancakes.

"I hope it's okay. I made you some breakfast too," Reese whispered. "Listen, Dane, I'm just as lost as you are in all this. It wasn't something I planned, either. If I overstep, just tell me."

"Thanks for breakfast, honey. And, as for your question, I became a firefighter because of my father." Dane shrugged as if talking about his father wasn't a big deal, but it was.

"Cole?" she asked. The toddler looked up at his mother and Dane couldn't help his chuckle.

"Mommy," Cole said, smiling at Reese.

"Yes baby," she answered her son, offering him another piece of banana. He shook his head and waved her off, shoving another bite of pancake into his mouth. Dane had to admit; he was a pretty cute kid.

"Yeah, my dad," Dane answered. "He was a firefighter and a damn good one," Dane boasted.

"You said he died when you were just a teenager, right?" Reese asked. This was the part Dane hated most when it came to talking about his dad. Whenever he had to explain that his father died on the job it always reminded him just how dangerous his job was. Really, that wasn't something he would ever forget and rightly so. Men who forgot how dangerous being a firefighter was usually ended up meeting the same fate as his dad had.

"Yeah, he died on the job," Dane whispered. Reese's gasp said it all. She quickly understood what he dealt with on a daily basis.

"I'm sorry, Dane," she said.

"Thanks." He shrugged as if it wasn't a big deal but even after all these years, it still was. "It's part of the job and I knew that going in but it still stings. He passed when I was a teen and that was hard. I needed a father and he wasn't around to help me figure things out. My mother did the best she could, but I wasn't the easiest teenager," he admitted.

"Yeah, I'm not looking forward to when Cole is going through his unruly teen years," Reese said.

Dane groaned, "If he turns out to be anything like me then I need to apologize now." Reese giggled and he felt a little lighter. He hated talking about such dark stuff especially just before a shift. It made him consider all of the things that could go wrong and that was the last thing he needed playing on a loop in his mind while he was on the job.

Still, one thing was bothering Dane and he had to ask. "Why did you pick my dad's name?" Dane asked.

Reese's smile lit up the room and Dane felt as though he was holding his breath, waiting for her to speak. "That night," she started; making a face to let him know that she was talking about that night. Dane smiled and nodded, letting her know he was picking up on her not so subtle hint. "You mentioned him when I asked about your tattoo. When I figured out he was yours, I decided to give him something of you. Your tattoo was one of the only things I remembered from our night together," she grimaced at her admission. "Sorry," she offered.

"You were pretty gone," Dane said. "But it does hurt that my tat is all you remember," he admitted, bobbing his eyebrows at her causing her to giggle.

"I remember bits and pieces but for some reason, that conversation really stuck with me. It seemed like a no brainer when the results came back that David wasn't Cole's dad." Reese took a bite of the banana she had given up on feeding to Cole. She seemed to be considering her next words carefully and Dane waited her out.

"About my offer to submit to a DNA test to prove Cole is your son, it stands. I will do whatever you need for me too, but I need for you to know I would never lie about something like this. Cole is the most important person in my life and I would never introduce you to him if I wasn't one hundred percent sure." Reese grabbed some of the dirty dishes from the table and started filling the sink with warm soapy water.

"I appreciate it, Reese," Dane said. "I'll give it some thought." He stood and took the rinsed plate from her hands noting her breathy little gasp when his fingers brushed over her wet, soapy hand. "I'll dry," he whispered.

"Don't you have to go to work?" she asked.

"I have a little time before I have to be down to the station," Dane said. They worked in silence while Cole sat up to the table, eating and humming to himself. He seemed so content, Dane was fascinated by the fact he was the same kid as the one he met last night. He was pretty sure the screeching toddler who had a meltdown in his spare room last night couldn't be the same boy sitting at his breakfast table this morning.

"He seems like a happy little guy," he whispered, not wanting to distract the toddler. "You've done a good job with him," Dane said. He couldn't imagine being a single parent and having to do it all alone. He had to hand it to Reese; she seemed like one tough woman. He could have guessed it about her given the fact she picked herself up and still went on her honeymoon even after her groom left her at the altar. But to raise a kid all on her own took being a badass to a whole new level.

Reese nodded and smiled, seeming to soak up Dane's praise. "Thanks," she said. "He's been a handful, I won't lie. But, I wouldn't change one minute with him. He drives me crazy and keeps me completely sane, all at the same time—if it makes any sense.

Dane laughed, "Not really but then I've never really been around any kids. My friend Jace will be a dad in a few months, but none of my friends have children yet."

"I guess they'll all be pretty surprised you're a dad," Reese asked. Dane groaned at the thought of having to tell his friends he fucked up and got a woman pregnant. Jace had ridden his ass for months now to get his shit together and stop screwing around with women who couldn't offer him more than one night of hot sex. He never admitted to his friends he was feeling the same way. Dane kept the fact he hadn't been with a woman for a few months now to himself. Telling Jace he was right often led to a whole lot of boasting on his friend's part. Jace would be unbearable to be around if he knew about Cole.

"Yeah, I'm not looking forward to the conversation," Dane admitted. "My mother will be thrilled. She's been bugging me to settle down and have kids for years now," he said, glancing over at Cole again. He wondered just how long it would take for his mother to try to shove him and Reese together. His mom was going to be disappointed she wasn't getting the whole package deal.

"So, you've never settled down then? There's no special woman you are going to have to do some explaining to?" Reese didn't look at him, seeming fixated on cleaning the same plate for the last few minutes.

Dane took it from her hands, "No," he said. "No special woman," he confirmed.

"Ah, still playing the scene then," she assumed. "Please tell me your cheesy pick-up lines have improved." Reese giggled and he found her assumptions a lot less funny.

"Not really," he said. He wanted to tell her he had changed but a few months of lying off of the local dating scene really didn't count as a hardcore life adjustment. "I've been laying low. You know, working on getting into the local station and becoming a fireman. I just haven't had much time for dating," he explained.

Part of it was true; he didn't really have time to go out to the local bar and troll for women. He left out the part where he really had no interest in that lifestyle anymore. He was ready for a change, but he wasn't sure just what that would look like. One thing was becoming perfectly clear to him—his sordid past looked like it had finally caught up to him and he worried the change he was looking for was going to knock him completely on his ass.

Reese

Reese wasn't sure how she felt about the whole domestic scene which played out that morning between her and Dane. Hell, it felt normal having breakfast just the three of them and she was having trouble focusing every time she chanced a look up at Dane. She had forgotten just how good looking he was and when his fingers grazed her hand she felt the same damn sparks she had their one and only night they spent together.

"How about you?" Dane asked. Reese handed him the last breakfast dish and she chanced a look up at him.

"Sorry, what?" she asked.

"Did you meet anyone and settle down?" he asked. Reese couldn't help her laugh; really did he not see the toddler smearing pancakes onto the table covered in syrup?

"Sure, I have guys lining up to take me out." She laughed at just how untrue that was. "They see my kid and they run in the other direction," she said. "Most guys in New York want easy, no-strings relationships. I don't offer any of those things, so it's easier to concentrate on Cole and my career." She knew she sounded like a cold bitch, but she wouldn't sugarcoat the truth.

She was alone, well except for her son and that was fine with her. She wanted to concentrate on being a good mom and making a name for herself as a lawyer with any free time she had left in her day.

"What do you do, you know—up in New York?" Dane asked. She hesitated, not sure she wanted to share too many personal details with him yet. She was leery of letting someone in because she wasn't a fan of being hurt or worse, disappointed. Dane looked like someone who could make her feel both of those things so she'd held her hand close to her vest—for now.

"I'm a lawyer," she admitted.

Dane whistled. "Well, I guess it makes sense," he said.

"How so?" she questioned.

"When you got here you said you weren't here for the money. I assumed you were either from a well off family or had a good job," he said.

"Both," she whispered. God, she hated admitting these types of things to people. In New York, she was part of an elite group, but in no way close to the level of some of the city's major power players. Her father made sure she hung around people with the same social status, never letting her slum it, as he liked to say. He wasn't exactly happy about the fact that his grandson's father was a lifeguard; he had a fit when he found that out. He would consider Dane a blue-collar, not worth his time, kind of guy. Reese had to admit a part of her liked that she defied her father by just spending one night with Dane. She never really thought of her reasoning behind making Dane the offer she did three years ago, but maybe him admitting he was a lifeguard had something to do with it.

"So, why not go to your family for help then?" he asked. "Why come all the way down here and risk telling me Cole is my son?"

Reese had good reason, but she worried telling Dane might just get her and her son booted out onto the street. She had no choice but to tell him the truth, she owed him at least that for the way he so easily let her and Cole into his life. Dane could have just as easily sent them packing but he didn't.

"My family might be the people who I'm running from," she admitted. "It's a long sordid story and I promise to tell you everything when you have the time." Dane checked his watch and nodded.

"Sorry, but I do need to head out," he said. "Are you sure you two will be good here until I get done my shift? I should be home around six." Reese thought it was sweet Dane worried about the two of them, but honestly, she just needed some time to think things through. She needed to figure out her next move before it was decided for her. Whoever was after her and Cole always seemed to be one step ahead of her. She needed to regroup and strategize what she needed to do next. Reese just hoped like hell no one followed her to the island.

"Yes, we will be fine. Do you mind if I use your washer? I'm out of clean clothes." Reese took for granted the daily luxuries she was usually afforded. Not having any clean clothes was probably the one thing she missed most. Well, that and a bed to sleep in since she and Cole had spent the past week sleeping in her car. Last night was the first real rest she had had in days and it was heaven.

"Sure, help yourself. I don't have to tell you to stay in the condo and lock up when I leave?" he asked. Reese's heart did a little flip- flop when he smiled down at her. Honestly, she needed to remember what her relationship was to Dane or she was going to go and do something stupid, like fall for him. Reese had a feeling it would be easy to do given the way her body responded to him with every brush of his fingers over her skin. Or the way her heart raced each time he gifted her with his sexy half-smile. She was just a one night stand who ended up getting herself pregnant and Reese would do well to remember her place.

Cole had taken a longer than usual nap giving Reese plenty of time to get done all their laundry, find enough of what she needed in Dane's pantry and refrigerator to make her favorite chicken and pasta dish and even have time to clean his entire condo. She felt like such a burden showing up on his doorstep unannounced. Reese figured the least she could do was clean his place and make him a home-cooked meal.

She collapsed on the sofa and was just about asleep when she heard a soft rap on the front door. She wasn't sure what the protocol was for answering the door at a virtual stranger's house while he was at work. No one she knew would look for her at Dane's place and if they were it wouldn't end well for her and Cole if she chanced to answer the door. She hesitantly peeked out the peephole finding a gorgeous blonde standing on the other side of the door.

Reese rolled her eyes. Of course, Dane lied to her when he said he wasn't seeing anyone. Like he would just forget the blonde bombshell standing on the other side of the door, looking as if she had just stepped out of a fashion magazine with her business suit and heels Reese knew cost more than her rent in New York. She knew the type of woman who stood on the other side of the door. Frankly—she was that woman, or she used to be. Now, Reese was desperately trying to escape who she had become, if not for herself than for her son. One thing was certain, Dane had a type and the old Reese fit into the mold perfectly.

The blonde knocked again, this time with a little more force and Reese was sure her banging would wake Cole. She was hoping to get a quick nap in before her barrel of energy woke up and if her unwanted guest didn't stop trying to beat down the door, he'd be up sooner than she wanted. Reese sighed and unbolted the door leaving the chain in place to send a clear cut message to the woman. She wasn't in the mood for any company and the sooner she could get the blonde to hit the road, the sooner she could curl back up onto Dane's comfy sofa.

"Dane's not here now," she whispered. "You'll have to hook up with him later," Reese said. She noticed the amusement in the woman's eyes as she smiled back at her and Reese was sure that getting her to leave wasn't going to be so simple.

"I like you," the woman said. Honestly, Reese didn't give a fuck how the woman felt about her; she just wanted to be left alone.

"Thanks," Reese spat. "Now, go away." The woman threw her head back and full-on laughed just as Reese was about to shut the door. Instead, she couldn't take her eyes off the blonde. She had to be completely crazy, standing there laughing at Reese like a lunatic.

"Oh, you are going to give him hell, aren't you?" the woman asked. "I can't wait to watch this whole thing play out," she said. Reese wasn't sure what to say because honestly, the poor woman wasn't making much sense.

"I'm not here to see Dane. I'm actually here to meet you. My name is Toni Bernston," she said, trying to shove her arm through the small opening to shake Reese's hand.

Reese made no move to open the door, even with Toni's hand and wrist shoved through the crack. "So you know Dane?" Reese asked.

"Yep," Toni admitted. "He's one of my closest friends. He called to tell me about you being here and well, I thought I'd stop by to see for myself." Toni pulled her hand back through the door waiting for Reese to make the next move.

"See what for yourself?" Reese questioned, suddenly feeling like a sideshow freak. Honestly, what did Dane do, leave his condo and call everyone he knew to announce he had a woman and her kid staying at his place?

"I came to see the woman who has my friend so tied up in knots he's asking to bring a plus one to my wedding." Toni smiled and Reese wasn't following again. She must have looked as confused as she felt. "I'm sorry, Reese, is it? I'm not explaining this all very well, am I?" Reese shook her head.

"How do you know my name?" she asked.

"Dane told me all about you and Cole. By the way, it's really sweet you named him after Dane's dad. I didn't know his father personally but I hear he was a really great guy. Anyway, Dane told me about the two of you staying with him and I thought I would come over to see if you needed anything." Toni seemed to have one speed and Reese was having trouble keeping up.

"Are you always like this?" Reese asked. Toni laughed and Reese wasn't sure if it was a good or bad thing the woman found her so funny.

"No," Toni said. "I've had way too much coffee and honestly the last minute wedding problems that keep popping up are really wearing me down. Would you mind if I come in?" Toni asked. Reese wasn't sure if she should trust the woman or send her packing.

"Listen, if you'd rather I leave—" Toni offered.

"No, it's fine," Reese whispered. "We will just have to be quiet since my son is sleeping," she said. Toni nodded and Reese removed the chain letting her into the condo.

"Thanks," Toni breathed. "My feet are killing me." She pulled off her designer heels and threw them into the corner of the entryway. "I've been dying to do that all day," she said.

Reese followed her into the family room and watched as the woman made herself at home, sliding onto Dane's sofa and putting her feet up. "I hope this is okay," she asked.

"Sure," Reese said. "It's not my place so do whatever." She sat on the other end of the sofa keeping a watchful eye on Toni, waiting for her to make the next move. Reese could tell the woman was there on a mission; just what it entailed was still a mystery.

"So, how did you and Dane meet?" Toni asked.

Reese smiled. "You came here for information then," she said. "Did Dane send you or did you decide to come here on your own?" Reese asked. The thought of Dane sending a stranger over to question her pissed her off, but she would have probably done the same thing if she was in his shoes.

"Fuck no, Dane didn't send me. If he knew I was here he'd wring my neck," Toni admitted. "Honestly, I came over because I'm curious."

"About?" Reese sounded defensive, but she wasn't about to let her guard down.

"Well, I was dying to meet the woman who has Dane completely tied up in knots," Toni said. Reese shot her a skeptical look, causing her to giggle. "Whether or not you know it, Reese you totally have my friend tied up. It's something I've never seen before and if I was a betting woman I would have never bet against Dane being a confirmed bachelor for the rest of his life. But then you showed up on his doorstep yesterday and this morning he called me for advice—about you." Reese wasn't sure what the big deal was.

"I don't get why this is such a shock," Reese admitted.

Toni barked out her laugh again, "Dane has never talked to me about a woman—ever. I've known him for a while now and he's never called me up to tell me he had a woman at his place. And with a kid to boot? Well, let me just say we are all wondering how this all happened."

Reese smiled, "Well, we had sex and I wasn't on the pill at the time because I was just dumped at the altar. You know, that kind of thing doesn't really lend to a girl wanting to take her birth control because—well, what's the point right?" Reese knew she sounded like a complete smart ass but she really didn't care.

"Yeah, I really like you," Toni said.

Reese shrugged, "Okay," she sassed. Toni giggled again and Reese shook her head in disbelief. "Is there anything else you'd like to know—for curiosity's sake?" she asked.

Toni sobered and Reese regretted offering to answer any other questions. She had a feeling she wasn't going to like what Toni was going to ask next. "Are you here to hurt him or do you really need his help?" Toni held her hand up, effectively stopping Reese from answering. "I know you don't know Dane well and I also know he seems the type not to give a fuck but he does. If you are here trying to trick him or wanting to hurt him, I won't allow it," Toni said.

Reese opened her mouth to tell Toni to have a nice fucking life and to leave her alone, but she also knew it wouldn't help her case. She almost admired the woman for the way she stuck up for her friend. Reese couldn't remember the last time she knew for certain she could count on another person to stand up for her. She trusted a small group of women once and they ended up stabbing her in the back by sleeping with her fiancé.

After she got back from her singles honeymoon and found out she was pregnant with Cole, she cut everyone out of her life. But being alone left her with no friends having her back and ultimately landed her on a virtual stranger's doorstep, begging for help.

"I like you," Reese whispered, smiling at Toni. "Dane is a lucky guy to have a friend like you," she admitted. Toni's smile was easy and she sat back into the leather sofa.

"Yeah, I tell him that all the time but I don't think he gets it. Not like you do. I'll always have his back, that's what friends are for," Toni said.

"I used to believe that, but friends can also betray you," Reese whispered. "I'm not here to hurt him; he is my son's father. Sure, I need his help but I also want him to know his son."

Toni nodded, "Good to know," she said. "He tells me you're a lawyer. What's your specialty?" she asked.

"I practice business law—you know accusations, mergers, that type of thing. At least I did. I'm pretty sure my job won't be waiting for me if I ever return to New York," Reese said. Her father had all but written her off when she told him she was pregnant. He couldn't fire her and he knew it. The last thing her dear old dad would want is a lawsuit filed against his corporation for firing his daughter for getting pregnant. That's why she suspected he was trying to get to her through Cole. At least that was her hunch. Without much to go on, she could only speculate who was sending her threatening messages.

"Well, I own a development firm on the island and we are always looking for good lawyers. If you decide to stick around, let me know. Maybe we can work something out," Toni offered.

"Thanks, I'd appreciate it," Reese said. She hadn't given much thought as to where she would be tomorrow let alone months from now.

"Well, I have to get home. I have a final fitting on my wedding dress tonight and apparently, there is some cake emergency only I can fix," Toni said, rolling her eyes causing Reese to giggle. "I'd love for you and Cole to come to my wedding if you are free."

Reese nodded, not really knowing what to say to the kind invitation. She had literally met Toni moments ago and now she was inviting her and her toddler to a wedding. Reese hadn't been to a wedding since her own failed attempt and a part of her wanted to scoff at the idea. But, she was also smart enough to know marriage could work if both people were in love and committed to not sleeping their way through the bridal party.

"See you later, Reese," Toni said, pulling her in for a quick side hug.

"Um sure," she stuttered. Toni showed herself out and Reese locked up behind her. She wondered at just how different things were on the island, as opposed to her life back in New York.

The idea of sticking around for a while didn't seem like such a bad one, but that would mean giving Dane the chance to fall in love with his son and she worried she might be asking for too much. She didn't know how to be anything but a single mother and she wasn't sure if she would be able to share Cole. She was being completely honest with Toni; she wanted her son to get to know his father and the only way to do it was for her to give Dane the benefit of the doubt and a chance to be Cole's dad.

K.L. Ramsey

Dane

Dane had spent the day thinking about how his life had gone from predictable and almost boring to completely crazy in just twenty-four hours. He had gone on four minor calls and even had time to stop by his friend Nico's to have lunch with him and Toni. Honestly, he wanted to tell someone about Reese and he knew the two of them wouldn't judge him over his past decisions as Jace might. His ex-roommate had ridden his ass about laying off picking up women at the local bars, but Dane didn't listen. He hated being told what to do and it always felt like Jace's concern was accompanied by a lecture and it wasn't what Dane needed to hear.

He thought about going home for lunch to check in on Reese and Cole but he didn't want to seem too eager. Plus, he knew Toni and Nico might give him some much-needed perspective on how to handle the whole situation with houseguests. They told him to follow his heart, whatever the fuck that meant and Toni seemed a little too eager to invite Reese and Cole to her wedding. Dane wanted to tell her he wouldn't be bringing a plus one, but the knowing look on Toni's face made him think better of it. The thought of having Reese by his side, on an actual date, didn't scare the shit out of him. But, bringing someone to his friend's wedding would mean he was someone who dated and he didn't—ever. He knew that Toni would continue to push, so he caved and asked if he could bring Reese as his plus one—if she actually agreed to be his date. Dane knew that would be a stretch. Hell, she might be long gone before Toni and Nico's special day and then he wouldn't have to worry about the logistics of taking a date to their wedding.

When his shift was over, Dane found himself finding one excuse after another to avoid his condo. He had spent the day daydreaming about his and Reese's one night together, trying to remember every detail. Apparently, Reese was the one woman he had no problem remembering and his dick seemed to be on board for recreating every dirty scene that popped into his head. Dane knew having Reese in his bed again would be a huge mistake and now with Cole in the mix, he couldn't afford to make mistakes.

He ran out to the local diner for a burger and when he couldn't find any other reason to avoid Reese, he decided to man up and head home. Dane knew he was being a coward by avoiding having to face his past and well, frankly his future. He thought he was fine with the idea of having a son, but as the hours wore on he hid like a coward. He was going to have to face what was waiting for him back at his condo. It was time he faced the reality of the gorgeous woman and the kid they created together waiting for him back at his place.

By the time Dane finally got home all the lights were off and he had a moment of panic believing that Reese had taken Cole and left; even after finding her backpack still lying on the floor by the front door. He dropped his gear in the front hall and padded back to the kitchen trying to be as quiet as possible. He needed a beer, shower, and bed—in that order.

"Hey." Reese was sitting at the table in the dark kitchen as if she was waiting up for him to come home.

"Fuck," he shouted. "You scared the shit out of me, Reese," he admitted.

"Well, I figured waiting for you like this would be good practice for when Cole tries to sneak in late," she said, flicking on the kitchen light. Dane blinked against the brightness and realized Reese was sitting in his kitchen in one of his t-shirts and panties.

"Nice shirt," he said.

Reese had the audacity to smile at him, looking down her own body and back up at him as if daring him to ask for it back. "Cole was a little excited about his bath tonight and I had to change. This was the closest thing I could find. Hope you don't mind," she teased.

"It's fine," Dane said. Hell, it was more than fine to find her sitting half-naked in his kitchen wearing just his t-shirt. He wanted to cross the room and pull her into his arms to kiss her senseless, just to show her how fine he thought the whole thing was, but it would be crossing a line.

"So, you were waiting up for me?" Dane asked. He wasn't going to lie; he liked the idea of Reese taking enough interest in him to wait for him to get home. Dane was pretty sure that the last person to wait up for him was his mother and that was a fucking long time ago.

"Yeah, I was starting to worry about you," she admitted.

"Worry?" Dane questioned.

"Yes," she said, clearing her throat. "Well, your job isn't exactly the safest and I was worried that something happened to you today when you didn't come home after your shift." Her words instantly made him feel like a complete ass. Here he was wandering around town acting the coward and she was sitting back at his condo worried about him.

"I'm sorry, Reese," he whispered. "I didn't think—well, let's just say that I don't usually have someone waiting for me at home and no one has worried about me in a damn long time. I'll try to consider that next time. But, you have to know that my job isn't going to change. Being a fireman is dangerous work and something that you will have to get used to. I mean—you and Cole. Being his father won't change my career path and it's just something you'll have to accept." He wouldn't change who he was and what he loved doing, but he did hate to think of his son growing up without him in his life, much as Dane had to finish growing up without his dad. Reese and Cole would have to get used to the dangerous aspects of his occupation.

Reese nodded, "I know, Dane. I would never ask you to change who you are or what you do. But you have to understand that it is going to take me some time to get used to you putting yourself in danger every time you leave for work."

"Understood," he said. "Thank you, Reese." She shyly smiled at him and he wanted to touch her but he knew that would be a mistake.

"I made you some dinner," Reese whispered. "I can warm it for you if you'd like." She stood and Dane just about swallowed his tongue, getting the full effect of just how much of her curvy, sexy body was left uncovered by his shirt. If she got any closer he wouldn't stop himself from touching her and doing all the things he thought about doing to her all day long.

"Thanks, but I grabbed a burger while I was out tonight," he admitted. Dane didn't miss the flash of disappointment that crossed Reese's face and he wondered what she was thinking.

"I get it, Dane. You have a life and Cole and I being here can't be easy for you. I don't want to cramp your style," she whispered and turned to go back to her bedroom.

Dane was feeling a little dizzy from her complete one-eighty. One minute she's taunting him in his t-shirt and making him dinner and the next she was pissed he had a burger and stayed out late. Dane grabbed her arm effectively stopping her from going back to her room and Reese gasped out her surprise.

"Hold up, honey. You wanna tell me why you're so pissed off at me all of the sudden?" He pulled her back to stand in front of him wanting to be able to see her. Hell, he knew it made him a masochist but he didn't care. He was used to being a little tortured, but Reese took his pent up desires to a whole new level.

"I'm not pissed, Dane. Heck, I'm not even angry. I know the score with you. I'm just sad you don't want better for yourself. You haven't changed in the three years since we last saw each other," she accused. Reese pointed her little finger into his chest and instead of being hurt or angry about what she was saying to him, he felt hot, bothered and a whole fucking lot turned on.

He grabbed her hand and held it against his chest. "Why don't you tell me how I haven't changed, honey," he teased. He could tell by the catch in her breath she was turned on by the whole scene too, but Reese was a lot smarter than he was, or maybe she was into self-preservation because she pulled her hand free and took a step back from him.

"I just thought you'd want more than a quickie in a hotel room by now," she whispered.

"Honey, there was nothing quick about our time in your hotel room," he taunted. He liked the way Reese's eyes flared at his mention of their night together.

"Well, I just, I um-" Reese stammered and he didn't hide his smile. She was pretty fucking adorable when she was tongue-tied and flustered. Dane reached out and grabbed her hand again not making a move to pull her any closer. He just wanted some sort of contact with her. Reese shivered and linked their fingers together, seeming to crave their connection too.

"Hmm, I wonder?" Dane didn't hesitate, pulling Reese into his body and crushing his lips against hers. She sighed into his mouth, leaning into his body and Dane instantly knew the same damn sparks he remembered from their night together were still there. He thought about how she made his body tingle with need every time she touched him that night, three long years ago, and he wondered how she was the only woman to ever make him feel that way. Touching her now, kissing her, made him remember everything about their night together and he wanted more. He wanted everything—he wanted Reese.

Dane ran his hands down her curves and grabbed handfuls of her luscious ass, cupping and squeezing, loving the way she moaned into his mouth seeming to need more from him. She broke their kiss leaving him needy and panting.

"We can't do this, Dane," she whispered. She was still wrapped up in his arms, her forehead resting against his chest, sharing the same air as him. Reese made no move to untangle herself from his hold and he knew she didn't mean a fucking word of her protest for him to stop, but he wouldn't push her for more. He wanted Reese to want him just as much as he needed her but he wouldn't push and he wouldn't beg.

"I won't be sloppy seconds," she said. Her accusation stung and he released her.

"What the fuck does that mean, Reese?" he questioned.

"It means you were out all evening with God only knows who and I won't be the woman waiting for you to come home after you're finished with your booty call," she spat.

Dane laughed, "Well, I see you have already decided who I am, Reese. Tell me, why are you here if I'm such a bad guy?"

"You know why I'm here; I need your help," she said. God, he wanted her to want to be there with him because she wanted to be and not because she had no other options. He knew it was crazy but he wanted Reese to want him. She was only using him to help her keep Cole safe and he needed to remember that.

"Fine, so you just need me to help you figure out who is trying to hurt Cole and get to you?" he questioned. "Duly noted counselor," he almost shouted. "Let's not waste any more time then. The sooner we can solve this mystery, the sooner you can be on your way." Dane knew he was acting like an ass but he didn't give a fuck. She hurt him and his knee jerk reaction was to give as good as he got. Right now, she was giving it to him pretty damn good.

"Alright," she shouted, crossing the room to sit back down at his table. "Let's get everything out in the open, Dane. Do you want to know who's after me? Well, I have a pretty good hunch it's my dear old dad. And here's the kicker—he wants to hurt me because I spent the night with you. Hell, he wanted to make me pay for giving birth to Cole because I slept with a blue-collar nobody, low life." Dane sunk down into the chair across from her. Her words felt like a personal attack.

"Your own father wants to hurt Cole?" he whispered.

"Yes," she admitted. "At least, I think it's who has been sending me those letters," she confirmed.

"Do you think I'm all of those things, Reese?" Dane hated asking her. He worried she would be of the same mindset as her father and Dane didn't know if he could handle it. He knew it was crazy he cared so much what Reese thought about him but he did. She was his son's mother. Hell, she was more than that to him, but he was pretty sure admitting that truth would lead to him losing his heart to the woman sitting across the table from him and that couldn't happen.

Hellfire

Reese

She watched Dane as he waited for her answer and God, she wanted to go to him and reassure him she didn't feel the same way as her asshole father did. She didn't care about any of that crap, but the way Dane watched her told her he did. He cared if she thought he wasn't good enough for her or even worse if she thought he wasn't good enough to be Cole's dad.

He shrugged, hiding his hurt with his smile but Reese could still see his disappointment. "Maybe your father's right to feel like that about me. Hell, up until a few months ago I was still hooking up with women, offering them one night but nothing more. You knew who you were falling into bed with, Reese." His tone sounded almost like an accusation and she hated that the night had come down to them sitting across Dane's kitchen table arguing about whether he was a decent human being or not. He took her and Cole in, no questions asked and that had to count for something. In Reese's book that alone made him a pretty fucking awesome person.

"Wait—you haven't had a one night stand in months?" she asked. Of course, it was what her brain would focus on. She was furious with Dane when he didn't come home after his shift. About mid-day, he texted he was going to be done work and home by dinner. At first, she thought he might have had to go out on a call and the amount of worry she felt for him made her realize she might care more for Dane than she wanted. Reese knew his job as a firefighter would land him in dangerous situations, but she never imagined worrying about him the way she did all day.

After Reese bathed Cole and got him into bed she decided to wait up for Dane hoping her instincts were wrong because her head was screaming at her he was with another woman. And, why wouldn't he be? Dane owed her nothing especially not an explanation. She was the one who just showed up in his life yesterday unannounced. Hell, she didn't know if he had a girlfriend or a wife. For all she knew he could have found himself a woman and settled down with kids and the whole nine yards. She breathed a sigh of relief finding he was single and alone and it was crazy because she didn't want anything from Dane except his help to keep their son safe. At least that was what she told herself. But the way he kissed her made her feel things she hadn't felt in years—three years to be exact.

Dane's smile was mean and she regretted asking him another personal question. She needed to learn his business wasn't her own even with him being her son's father. Reese had no hold on him and no right to ask Dane questions about where he had been all night. He had already made it perfectly clear to her.

"I know you have already decided what I was doing tonight, honey, but you were wrong. Sorry to burst your bubble, but I had a burger and then came home." Dane eyed her across the table and she could tell from his expression he was lying. He had the same look on his face Cole got when he did something wrong and then told her he didn't.

"You know, you and your son get the same look on your faces when you aren't being honest," she whispered. She wished she didn't have to call him on his shit but the lawyer in her wanted answers. Reese needed to get to the bottom of where Dane was and who or what he was doing. It was the only way she felt she could move forward and trust him.

"Please just be honest with me, Dane. I just want your honesty if you can't give me anything else." She waited him out and felt about ready to self-combust when he gave her his knowing sexy smirk.

"Is that all you want from me, honey? Just my honesty?" He so easily turned the tables on her; she was really going to have to stay on her toes if she wanted to keep up with Dane. It didn't help her case that he turned her girl parts to mush every time he walked into the same damn room as her.

"Right now, yes," she admitted. "I can't afford to take chances with Cole and I won't be caught up in the middle of something. If you're seeing someone or you are still into one-night hook-ups, what just happened can't ever happen again." Reese motioned to where they had had their scorching kiss.

"You mean we can't kiss again if I'm hooking up with other women?" Dane questioned. Reese hesitated. She didn't want it to sound so final, but she was sure if she gave Dane the power to, he'd break her heart and that couldn't happen, not now—she wasn't strong enough.

Reese nodded, "Right," she confirmed. "I can't let myself fall for your charms again, Dane. If you're only out for one night stands and cheap hook-ups then consider my lips off-limits." Reese watched Dane looking for some sign he was even interested in kissing her again. She assumed from the scorching kiss he just gave her that he wanted her, but she wasn't so sure now.

"Fine," Dane agreed. He stood and Reese was sure he was going to leave the room and just be done with her, but instead he pulled her up from her chair and sealed his mouth over hers again. His tongue demanded access and at first, she refused him. But when Dane snaked his hands down her body to cup her ass in his big hands she couldn't help her gasp. Reese's lips parted allowing Dane to lick his way into her mouth. By the time he finished kissing her, she was breathless with need and her body was humming with desire.

"I'm not sure if that answers your question, honey but I'm not seeing anyone. I haven't been with a woman in months and I wasn't planning on hooking up with anyone for just a night. I know this must be hard for you to believe, but the reason I didn't come home tonight after my shift was because I'm a chicken shit." Dane smiled at her and it damn near took her breath away again. She wanted to believe him because then she could cling to the foolish hope he might want her again. For three years now, she had been dreaming of the man who stole a little piece of her heart and gave her so much more in return— Cole.

She knew she was romanticizing what she and Dane shared but it was all she had to work with. She had been out on a few dates, but once she got to the part of the evening where she felt the need to share she had a son; her date would mysteriously have to cut their date short never to be heard from again. She was embarrassed to admit Dane was the last person she slept with. The only personal relationship Reese had was with her vibrator and it was a fact she would just keep to herself.

"What do you mean? You were afraid to come home knowing Cole and I were here?" Reese hated that she was driving Dane from his own home but she didn't know why he'd fear facing her. If anything, she should be the one afraid to face him. She was the one who kept the fact he had a son from him.

"I think I was more afraid to come home and find you both gone," Dane sighed and sat back down into his chair pulling her along with him to sit on his lap. She didn't want to cuddle into his hold after he wrapped his big arms around her middle but her traitorous body seemed to crave the connection.

"When you showed up here yesterday all I wanted to do was shove you back out my front door and go back to bed. And yet, I just spent the entire day at work thinking about you and Cole being here and I was actually looking forward to coming home for the first time in a very long time. The closer it got to the end of my shift, the more I panicked. I was afraid that I might come home to find an empty condo and the thought scared the shit out of me," Dane whispered.

"You like us being here?" Reese questioned. She had spent the whole day worried he was going to come to his senses and kick the two of them out and she really had no plan B.

Dane chuckled, "Yeah, I think I do," he breathed. "Hell, I even stopped over at my friend's house and told them all about you," he admitted.

Reese nodded, "Toni stopped by here this afternoon."

"Fuck, sorry," he said, shooting her a sheepish grin. "I told her to stay the hell away from you. She's a little much."

Reese giggled, "Yeah, she is. But it was nice the way she stuck up for you. She loves you and doesn't want you to get hurt. I showed up here out of the blue claiming Cole is your son.

Toni was just being a good friend. You're lucky to have someone like her in your life." Reese felt an unexplained sadness at the realization she had no one in her life that would go to bat for her if she were in a bind. It was her and Cole against the world and it got to be a bit lonely if she was being completely truthful.

"Do you have someone like that in your life?" Dane whispered. He was so perceptive she wasn't going to be able to hide from him the way she did everyone else.

"No," Reese admitted. "I thought I did, but it turned out people were in my life because of my social status and money, not because they wanted to be my friend. Even my own fiancé used me to get into my father's company," Reese said. After she got back from her singles honeymoon, she decided to stop wallowing in her own self-pity. She picked herself up, dusted off the lust-filled haze Dane had created around her from their only night together and went back to work. Her father called her into his office to explain that just because she chose not to follow through with her wedding, things around the office were going to be business as usual. He wasn't about to fire David just because she didn't want to be married to him. Hell, her father even went as far as siding with her ex-fiancé, telling her that she created the mess in her life and now she would have to face the consequences daily.

"Wait, you work with your ex?" Dane asked. She nodded, knowing just how messed up it all sounded.

"He works for my father's firm and my dad said he was a valuable asset to the company. In fact, he basically said if he had to choose, he'd choose David since he brought in the most clients and well, earning power." Reese laughed at just how messed up it sounded.

"What kind of father picks the guy who cheated on his daughter over his own flesh and blood?" Dane asked. Reese didn't have an answer to his question. Since having Cole, she couldn't imagine putting anyone else's needs before her son's.

"It was business," she said. "It hurt but I understood. He told me if I wanted to stay with the firm, I'd have to be a team player and David was on my team. It wasn't easy to see him day in and day out. David was a reminder I failed; I was lacking in some way and he had to find what he needed elsewhere." Dane's arms tightened around her body and he pulled her back against his chest.

"No fucking way, honey," he growled against her neck. "There is no fucking way you are lacking in any way, shape or form," Dane said. Reese appreciated that he felt that way, but his opinion was based on one night not years in a relationship.

"It's not a big deal, Dane," she whispered. "David and I were together for a few years and well, I guess I became complacent. He grew tired of hearing that I couldn't go out because I was working on a brief or I didn't want to have sex because I was studying for the bar. David was a few years older than me and when he was hired onto the firm, he decided to make some of his own fun while I was busy trying to build my career." Reese left out the part where he slept his way through the office paying special attention to her friends and the women who would later become her bridesmaids. She had no clue he was making her the laughing stock of the company.

"I later found out my father knew David was sleeping his way through my friends and he said nothing. He told me it was what guys do and I should count myself lucky David was still willing to marry me," Reese said. "Well, until my best friend convinced him I wasn't worth the trouble and they left my wedding together. That was why I ended up down here. I found out the two of them had been sleeping with each other and when I called off the wedding, they ran off together."

"Fuck," Dane cursed. "You had some real fucking winners for friends, baby." She learned friends were hard to come by once she tried to make her way back into society. She was shunned and even uninvited to local events once news got out about her pregnancy. It became common knowledge David took a paternity test after Cole was born and he wasn't the father. People started to whisper about who they thought the father was and somehow her secret got out that Cole was the product of a one night stand.

"When I found out I was pregnant I went to the only person I thought I could trust, my father. I was starting to show and I knew I was in a race against time. He couldn't fire me for being pregnant. What kind of monster would that have made him?" Reese asked. "He told me there was still time. He said he could make David do the right thing and leave my former best friend to marry me."

"Well, that was big of him," Dane said. "I hope you told him to fuck off?" he asked.

Reese laughed at the idea of telling her father to fuck off. "No," she admitted. "I did the next best thing though, I told him about you. When he found out someone besides David might be the father, he was outraged. He even had the nerve to ask me how I could cheat on David."

"You didn't," Dane said. She liked the way he jumped in to defend her but it was so long ago.

"I know, but my father lives in his own world," Reese said. She knew the score, her father would always side with David and it felt like a knife to the gut. That was the day she decided she could only depend on herself. She was all alone and Reese realized that worked for her. She was going to figure her life out and raise her baby on her own.

"I told my father I didn't need David or anyone else's help; that I'd raise my baby on my own and he laughed at me. He told me if I went through with the pregnancy, he'd fire me."

"I'm no lawyer, but isn't that illegal?" Dane asked. Reese smiled and nodded up at him.

"Yep, and I took great pleasure in reminding him of the fact. He had his human resource department hound me for months and I eventually had to hire my own lawyer to fight all the bogus accusations he lobbed at me. When my father realized I wasn't going anywhere he gave up trying, but he wrote me off in every other way possible," Reese admitted.

The pain of being disowned by her own family was the worst. Her mother had stopped calling her to pretend she was interested in any aspect of Reese's life and her father ignored her. She became invisible in her own family and for a while, she wasn't sure if she was going to be able to afford to stay in the city. Her father was paying part of her rent after David moved out. Rent control only went so far in Manhattan and she was afraid she'd be forced to either find a smaller place to live or move out of the city completely.

"My parent's cut me out of their lives and I almost lost everything. My father had black-balled me and I knew no other firm would hire me if I decided to switch firms. I was going to lose my apartment and I would have had nowhere to go. I was almost nine months pregnant and my only thought was I'd have this little baby depending on me and no means of being able to take care of him. I actually hoped David turned out to be my baby's dad because then my father would have accepted Cole as his grandson. He would have never let us live on the streets," she said.

"What happened?" Dane asked.

"Well, I turned twenty-five just before giving birth to Cole," Reese said. Dane looked at her as if she lost her mind. He didn't come from the world of old money and wouldn't really understand inheritance and trust funds.

She smiled up at him, "My grandfather was a very wealthy man," she offered. "When I turned twenty-five I got my trust fund from his estate and there wasn't a damn thing my father could do about my inheritance and believe me—he tried. He tried to keep me tied up in litigation for months and finally, the judge ruled in my favor. I was able to escape eviction from my apartment and I became a wealthy woman. In fact, I don't have to work another day in my life if I don't want to." She shrugged like it was no big deal, but judging from the look on Dane's face, it was.

"So, did you quit your job?" he asked.

"Nope," she admitted. "There was no way I was going to let my father push me out of my job. Believe it or not, I love my work. Sure, working for my father wasn't a walk in the part but seeing him squirm every time I walked into the board room was," she admitted. Dane threw back his head and laughed and Reese felt as though her entire world had become a little brighter. Dane was so easy to talk to and be with, she wondered if he would understand this next part or if he'd turn her away.

"The threatening letters started about the time I received my inheritance. At first, I thought it was just someone wanting money but they never demanded cash. They never really asked for anything, just made nasty threats. The last letter I received, the one I showed you yesterday, threatened Cole and I knew I had to do something. If they get their hands on my son," she whispered, not able to finish her sentence.

"Our son," Dane corrected. "And, they will have to go through me first," he growled. It felt good to have someone on her side. She knew Dane would keep his word and not let anyone get to Cole, but hearing him call Cole his did crazy things to her heart.

Reese straddled his lap and wrapped her arms around his neck. "Thank you, Dane. You are going to be an amazing father and I'm so sorry I kept you in the dark about Cole. I just didn't know what to do."

Dane shook his head and Reese worried he was going to give her a hard time about not telling him about the baby, but what he said instead threw her off her game. "I'm not sure I can be his dad," Dane whispered. Reese worried he would turn them away but if he didn't want Cole then he couldn't have her. Dane closed his eyes and Reese held her breath waiting for him to tell her they would have to find someone else to help them.

The problem was she had no one else to turn to. Dane was her last hope for finding out who was trying to get to her son.

Dane

"Why the hell did you give me hope if you have no intention of being a father to Cole? I can't take the chance he's going to get attached to you and then what? You just kick us to the curb?" Reese tried to get up from his lap and he banded his arms around her body, tugging her against his chest. There was no way he would let her run from him, not until he said exactly what he needed to say to her.

"That's not what I meant, honey," he whispered. "Just give me a chance to explain, please." Reese stopped squirming around on his lap and his cock protested, liking the way her sexy ass was rubbing all over him.

"Fine, but if you tell me you don't want a relationship with our son, I won't be able to stay here, Dane. I won't put him through getting to know you and then losing you," she whispered.

"I want to know him, Reese. I want to know both of you," he admitted. He decided he was done being a coward. He had spent most of the evening trying to come up with reasons why he wasn't good enough to be a part of his son's life, but none of them added up to equal the fact he was happy about Cole being his kid. He was cautious at first, but the more time he took to think about being a dad, the more he worried he wouldn't do a decent job of it.

"Then why can't you be his father? I don't understand," Reese admitted.

"I'm worried I'm going to do a shit job of it," she said. "God Reese, what if I fuck up and screw up our kid's life? Do you really want that for him?" Dane whispered. He hated being so unsure about his own abilities but the last thing he wanted was to screw up his own kid.

"Why do you think you'll be a bad father?" Reese questioned.

"My dad was great, but I lost him when I was just a teen. I lost out on so much time with him and now I'm starting late with Cole and I feel like I've missed out on so much of his life already. He doesn't know me, Reese," he said. Dane could tell she was going to say something, effectively interrupting him but he needed to get the rest out. He pulled her in for a quick kiss, stealing her argument.

"That's not on you, Reese. Honestly, it says a lot more about me and the man I was. We had a one night stand and I never even bothered to find out where you were or anything else about you. Hell, I would have wanted more than just one night with you. I couldn't get you out of my fucking mind for almost a year but I was too much of a coward to look for you. I can't explain it really but I've never thought of myself as worth sticking around for. I guess I didn't want to face rejection and one night with a woman usually was enough for me—until I found you," he admitted. Dane just hoped he wasn't telling Reese too much, playing his hand before it was even dealt.

"But, you just disappeared from my room that night," Reese accused. "I woke up the next day and you were gone."

Dane thought back to that night and the way she called him by her ex's name. It hurt and he was confused by the way she made him feel so he left before she even told him her last name. "You called me David," he whispered.

Reese covered her mouth, "I'm so sorry, Dane. I was drunk and I didn't know—I didn't mean to," she said. He knew that, but hearing Reese say it made him feel better.

"I know, but at the time I was an ass. It hurt and I left. I laid off the dating scene for a while telling myself I just needed a break, but honestly, I just wanted you. I know our night together screwed up your life back in New York, but I was pretty fucked up after you disappeared out of my life." God, saying it all out loud made him feel like a complete jackass. Why didn't he go after her or hire someone to track her down, as she did him?

"I'm so sorry, honey," Dane whispered. "I should have tried harder to find you. Hell, I should have been and done a lot of things but I fucked up. I finally gave up being the man that found you in the bar and took you back to your hotel room. I was done being him the night we met but it took me a while to figure that out. Even after I went back to the whole bar scene, it didn't seem to fit. I hooked up here and there but found that I had less time to troll bars with my new job's training schedule. Becoming a firefighter seemed to take over my life but in a good way. It's been months since I've even touched a woman," he admitted.

Dane had taken his best friend Jace's advice but he'd never admit it. Jace would gloat about being right and he'd never hear the end of it. Dane tried the whole one night stand thing after letting Reese walk out of his life but it never felt right again. He'd hooked up a few times, finding women on vacation or even a few locals to blow off some steam and have some hot, meaningless sex with. But a few months back, Dane saw how happy Jace was with Heather and thought why not? Why wasn't finding someone to settle down with in the cards for him too? He had decided to give up trolling the local bars for women and even thought about asking one out on a real date, but he'd never found anyone he wanted to take to dinner and get to know—not until now.

"Go out on a date with me, Reese?" he asked. He hated how desperate he sounded and he hoped like hell she didn't hear the same desperation in his voice.

"What?" she stuttered.

"Yeah, I want you to go on a real date with me—to dinner or a movie, I don't care. I just want my first real date since high school to mean something," he whispered.

Reese smiled at him and he felt his breath hitch in anticipation. He wanted her to say yes more than he wanted his next breath. "You haven't been on a date since high school?" she asked.

"Nope," he admitted. "I never wanted to get to know the woman in my bed. Well, not until now. I want to get to know you, Reese and I want to try to be Cole's dad if you'll both just give me a chance. I'm done being a coward and I'm done running away from what I want. I want you, Reese," he said. She didn't answer him and he thought she wasn't going to agree to his date, not with everything he just admitted to her. He wasn't really doing a bang-up job of convincing Reese to give him a chance.

"Okay," she said, nodding. Her beautiful smile was easy and he could tell she was being honest about letting him in; he just hoped like hell he wouldn't fuck it all up. "But what about Cole?" she asked. "I don't have a sitter on the island, and I don't want to leave him—you know, just in case." Reese was such a good mother and he hadn't really thought of all of the ins and outs of having a kid and finding a babysitter, but he knew exactly who he could ask and he knew for sure Cole would be safe.

"You met Toni?" he asked. Reese nodded. "Great, well tomorrow, I'll take you to meet her fiancé. He's as big as a hulk and I know they'd be happy to watch Cole for us for a few hours." Reese hesitated again and he waited her out.

"Alright," she conceded. "As long as you think he'll be safe, I trust you, Dane." Reese didn't know how much her trust meant to him. It was everything. She was giving him a chance with both her and Cole and now she was willing to trust him with their son's safety.

"Thank you, honey," he whispered against her mouth, pulling her in for a quick kiss. It was going to take every ounce of his will power to walk away from Reese tonight but he was going to. He didn't want her to end up in his bed, not tonight, not yet. He wanted to do things right with her this time. If he had to deal with his own blue balls to play the gentleman, he would.

"I think we should get to bed, Reese. We have a busy day tomorrow trying to figure out why your father would want to hurt our son and then go on our big date," he teased. Dane lifted her from his lap and tugged her down the hall, delivering her to her bedroom she shared with Cole. He didn't miss the flash of confusion in her eyes as he dipped his head to give her one more scorching good night kiss.

"I'll see you in the morning," he whispered against her lips.

"But," she stuttered in protest.

"But nothing, Reese. We are going to take this slowly and do things the right way this time. I wasn't kidding when I said I want a chance with both of you. I'm not going to fuck this up again," he whispered, not wanting to wake Cole. He reached around her body and opened her door. Dane turned to leave her standing there, to head back to his own room. He didn't dare turn around for fear of seeing all of Reese's pent up desire. She would have him changing his mind about walking away from her tonight. When he heard her sigh and her door quietly close, he almost wanted to chuckle, but with the way his cock was throbbing in his pants, it was too soon to find the whole situation humorous—maybe after a long, steamy shower it would be funny—maybe.

K.L. Ramsey

Reese

Reese slept like crap tossing and turning the entire night. Dane had gotten her all worked up and then basically deposited her at her bedroom door, turning down her not so subtle hints she wanted to end up in his bed; preferably underneath him panting out his name. Dane seemed to have other ideas about how their night should end. When he told her he wanted to take things slowly, she tried to protest but he shut her down. Really, she wanted to be angry with him for denying her but she didn't disagree with his reasoning. They were so quick to jump into bed together three years ago; Dane might be on to something with waiting to fall back into bed together now.

Cole hadn't woken her up at the break of dawn as he usually had. In fact, Reese woke up to a completely empty bed and room. She found a note from Dane taped to her nightstand telling her he had Cole and was feeding him breakfast. He ordered her to take the morning off and enjoy a bath or catch up on some sleep. Honestly, Reese couldn't decide which sounded better to her, but she knew she wouldn't be able to go back to sleep no matter how tired she was.

Reese stumbled into her bathroom and filled the tub with warm suds and brushed her teeth while she waited for the bath to fill. She stripped and sunk down into the warm bubbles and groaned at just how good it felt. She hadn't had a bath in ages. Usually, all Reese had time for was a quick shower and if she had a few minutes to shave her legs, she counted it as a win.

Reese could hear Cole giggling and smiled to herself. She had worried Dane and Cole wouldn't bond but giving them some alone time this morning seemed like a good thing judging from the silly noises and giggles coming from the kitchen. She hoped it meant Cole was getting to know his father and vice versa.

She had allowed herself to relax and lay back in the tub just in time for Cole to come barreling into the bathroom to find her. "Cole man, we need to let your mama sleep," Dane loudly whispered. He followed Cole into her bathroom and before she could react or even grab a towel, they were both standing over her. She tried to cover herself with the bubbles, but she was sure from the way Dane let his gaze wander over her body that she had missed a few patches.

"Sorry," he apologized; his eyes still not meeting hers.

"Um, can you hand me a towel?" she asked, nodding to the cabinet. "I'm naked here," she squeaked.

"Naked," Cole repeated. Her son had taken to repeating everything everyone around him said but wasn't much of a talker otherwise. Cole smiled up at Dane causing him to chuckle and Reese could feel her patience wearing thin, finding the whole scene a lot less funny.

"How about I take this little guy back out to finish his pancakes and bananas while you finish your bath?" Dane asked. She would never refuse more personal time and even thought about doing her hair and make-up for a change. If she was going to meet some more of Dane's friends and go on their date, she'd like to put her best foot forward.

Reese nodded her agreement. "Great," he said. Dane bent to kiss the top of her head and she could have melted into the tub from the sweet gesture. "I can't wait for our date," he whispered in her ear, causing her to shiver. Reese had to admit, she was pretty excited about their night out together too.

"Come on, little man," Dane said, snatching the toddler up and causing him to squeal. "Let's go eat some more pancakes and bananas." Reese watched as Cole vehemently shook his head in protest.

"No, no nanas," he shouted. Reese giggled at the way Dane was negotiating with her son. Sooner or later, he would come to realize negotiations were futile. Cole wasn't one to give in and when it came to eating fruits and vegetables; he usually dug his heels in and really gave her a fight. Reese was going to enjoy watching Cole give Dane some trouble, but she was pretty sure he'd be able to figure out their toddler.

Reese finished her bath and fixed her hair and make-up. When she finally wandered out to find Cole and Dane, the kitchen was clean and the two were sitting on the sofa watching an episode of an old cartoon. It was possibly the cutest thing she'd ever seen.

"Thanks for letting me sleep in and the bubble bath was amazing," she gushed.

"No problem, honey," Dane whispered. Cole was just about asleep on top of his chest and God, seeing her baby lying on his father that way did crazy things to her girl parts. Dane was hot, sure. But, seeing him interacting with Cole and now holding him while watching cartoons was downright sexy.

"You keep looking at me like that, Reese and I won't keep my promise to take things slow," Dane growled. Reese felt her own breath hitch at the thought of Dane making her his again. The last thing she wanted was for him to go slow about doing it, either. If she had her way, she would end up in his bed tonight after they put Cole to sleep, but she was afraid Dane would find her plan of action a little too aggressive. Reese knew he was worried about fucking the whole thing up between them, especially with Cole now in the mix but her overactive libido had plans—a whole lot of plans and all of them involved both her and Dane naked together.

"I can't help it, Dane. Seeing you with him, well—it's everything. Thank you," she whispered.

"He's my son and I want to know him, Reese. You don't ever have to thank me for being his dad. I should be the one thanking you for giving me a chance to know him," Dane whispered, stroking back Cole's hair from his face. She always thought her son looked like a little angel when he slept. When he was awake it was a whole different story. Her toddler was certainly learning his way around the world and that usually ended up with him spending some time in the timeout chair. It made her smile just thinking about some of the things he tried to pull. His newest stunt was putting his toys in the potty and trying to flush them down, usually leaving her with a clogged toilet and a huge mess to clean up.

"I left you some coffee and pancakes," Dane said. She realized he had been watching her and she suddenly felt shy.

"Thanks," she whispered, padding off to the kitchen. Reese knew she was feeling things for Dane that were better left alone between the two of them but she didn't care. She had spent the last three years feeling completely alone and often afraid of making the wrong move. Having Dane in her life and on her side felt right. She just hoped when she landed in his bed he'd still feel the same way about her and Cole hanging around. Reese knew if he walked away from her again it might break her heart and now she had Cole's heart to worry about too.

Hellfire

Dane

After Cole's nap, they decided to go into town so Reese and Cole could meet Nico. He was exhausted after his early morning wake-up call by the toddler, but he was still hoping Reese would want to go out on a real date with him. Hell, he was hoping she'd want more than just a date but he knew he had to take things slowly with her. Too much was at stake now with Cole and if he was being completely honest, he liked the idea of having them both in his life—long term. Even if that thought was foreign to him. He didn't usually want a woman past one night, but there was something about Reese that made him want more.

That morning, he woke up to Cole standing by his bedside watching him sleep and his first thought was to take him back to his room and Reese. When Dane realized it was only five-thirty and the sun wasn't even up, he felt a little guilty waking her. Reese had been through a hell of a lot lately judging by what she had shared with him last night. She needed her rest and it was about time he started doing his part with their son. He wanted to get to know Cole and what better way to do that then to just dive right into the deep end?

Dane got out of bed and changed Cole's diaper while the toddler leerily watched his every move. He couldn't blame him, as far as Cole was concerned he was a complete stranger. Dane turned on some cartoon network and found some of his old favorites for Cole to watch while he made some breakfast. He went with the safe bet and made pancakes again after seeing how much Cole seemed to enjoy them the prior morning. Dane even added some bananas and wanted to pat himself on the back for being a good parent—well, that was until Cole shot him death daggers for serving fruit with his beloved pancakes.

He couldn't get enough of his son and a part of him wondered if he'd ever be able to let Reese or Cole go again. Walking away from her three years ago seemed like the right thing to do. He couldn't get Reese out of his mind and he had been trying to find someone to fill the void she seemed to leave in her wake. Dane didn't want to admit it at the time, but he thought about their night together more often than he wanted. Reese bewitched him, in a good way and now that she was back in his life, he wasn't sure he would be able to walk away from her again.

When she let him kiss her last night he knew falling back into bed with her would be a huge mistake. He needed to slow down and take things easy with her; otherwise, she would get the wrong idea about what he wanted. He wasn't ready to admit it to anyone else but he wanted her to stick around. He wanted a chance to prove he wasn't the same asshole who hooked up with women and then walked away. Only time would prove that to her and Dane wasn't sure he'd have the time necessary to show her that he had changed. He worried as soon as he helped Reese solve her problem, she'd move back to New York with Cole and he wasn't sure he liked that idea.

They made it to Nico's in the early afternoon and Toni and Reese acted as if they were best friends, chatting and giggling. He liked the way Reese seemed to fit into his world. Cole took to Nico and didn't bother giving Dane a second look. It was almost comical watching his giant friend playing on the beach with the toddler.

When Reese let him know she felt comfortable leaving Cole with Toni and Nico, he kicked his plan to whisk her off to a romantic dinner into full gear. He decided to take her to the steak house that just opened and hoped she'd like his choice. He'd go anywhere really, as long as it was with Reese and she was happy. He hoped like hell she'd give him a chance to prove they could work. He also wanted to give her a break from being a mom and worrying about whoever or whatever was trying to get to her and Cole.

"I hope this is okay?" he asked nervously after they were seated.

Reese nodded enthusiastically causing him to chuckle. "I love steak," she whispered across the table as if she was sharing a secret with him. "I haven't had a good steak in ages."

"This place just opened down here so it's new for me too," he admitted. "I was hoping you liked steak. There is so much we don't know about each other and I want to know you, Reese." Her eyes met his and she gave him her shy smile. He loved this side of her. Reese seemed almost too capable; he wasn't sure where he would fit into her and Cole's lives. The more she allowed him in, letting him help with Cole, the more he seemed to find his way and his place with them.

"Well, I'm an open book. What would you like to know?" She smiled across the table at him and he felt his heart pounding in his chest. Maybe taking Reese out in public was a bad idea. The way he responded to her; the way his body seemed to need her had him rethinking not taking her back to his condo to put an end to his lust for her. But, Dane was sure taking what he wanted from Reese just once wouldn't be enough.

"Where do you see this going with us?" he asked. "I've told you I want a chance to get to know you and Cole but you haven't told me what you want from me, Reese," he said.

"I'd like to get to know you too, Dane. Right now, my life is so complicated, I'm worried about making you promises I won't be able to keep. What if my trouble in New York finds me here?

I won't be able to stay here knowing Cole is in danger." Dane reached across the table to take her hand into his needing contact with her.

"I wouldn't ever let anyone hurt our son, Reese," he promised. "I'd never let anyone get to either of you," he swore. Dane meant every promise he made her. There would be no way he'd let anyone get close enough to either of them to ever hurt them. "Tomorrow, we'll contact the local authorities to see what can be done about your letters." Reese nodded her agreement.

"I know you want for me to make you promise to tie whatever this is up into a nice neat package but I can't, Dane. I need to figure out the rest of my life first. I hope you can understand," she whispered across the table. He gave a curt nod letting her know he'd heard her, but honestly, he didn't understand any of this. Dane wasn't willing to let her go to give Reese time to figure out what was happening between the two of them. Losing Reese and Cole wasn't an option.

K.L. Ramsey

Reese

Reese hated that she seemed so indecisive when it came to answering what should have been a simple question. Her heart was screaming at her to tell Dane she wanted it all—everything he was willing to give her and so much more. She dreamed of sitting across a table from him, having a romantic dinner like the one they were currently having, for the past three years and she couldn't seem to get herself straight. She just wanted to make sure Dane understood how serious her situation was. She would never let anyone hurt her son and if it meant walking away from the only man she had been with or wanted in the past three years than she would. Reese wouldn't like having to do it, but she decided a long time ago that Cole was first in her life and it meant she wasn't able to make Dane any promises.

They spent the rest of the dinner getting to know each other. Every time he smiled at her or ran his thumb over her hand, she'd just about swallow her tongue. Wanting Dane wasn't a problem for her and if he'd just let her in, she would be in his bed tonight giving them both what they seemed to need. But every time she'd not so subtly bring up the topic of spending the night in his bed, he'd change the subject. Reese thought she was sexually frustrated before, but having Dane within touching distance was doing strange things to her girl parts.

"Dane Knight," a woman shouted from across the restaurant and Dane cringed. If Reese wasn't mistaken, he even rolled his eyes just before he stood to greet the older woman.

"Mom," he said, letting her pull him down for a bear hug. "You're choking me," he grouched.

"Well, that's because I never get to see you anymore and now that I finally get to wrap my arms around you, I want to do it right," his mother said. Reese giggled and Dane's mom looked at her and smiled. "And it seems that I've interrupted your lovely dinner. I'm so rude."

"No, not at all," Reese said. She stood and held out her hand. "I'm Reese Summers."

"I'm Gloria Knight, Dane's mom. But, you probably picked that up already. It's so nice to meet you, Reese," she said, giving her hand an extra squeeze. Reese wondered if Dane had already told his mother about her and Cole but from the deadpan look of fear on his face, she was sure he hadn't. She wasn't about to spill the beans on his behalf but wanted a front-row seat for the show while he did.

"Mom, you might want to sit down too. I have something that I need to tell you," Dane said. Gloria looked between the two of them and smiled, pulling out the chair between them and sitting down.

"Okay, let's have it, Dane. You have that same look you used to get when you got caught stealing cookies from the pantry too close to dinner. Out with it," she ordered. Reese knew immediately that she liked Dane's mother. She was a no-holds-bar kind of woman and Reese could get used to having her around. Plus, Cole was going to love having such a spunky grandmother. Her mother couldn't be bothered with her grandson and Reese hurt for her son, knowing that he would never have a warm, loving relationship with his grandparents. Gloria could be a game-changer though.

"I'm a father," Dane said, coming right out with his news.

"Geeze, Dane," Reese whispered.

"What?" he questioned.

"Well, you could have at least eased into it. I mean you didn't even give the poor woman a lead-in. You just put it all out there," Reese complained. Dane shrugged and looked back at his mother. Gloria seemed a little confused and there was something else that Reese couldn't seem to put her finger on, but if she had to give it a name, she'd say that his mother seemed excited.

"You mean to tell me that I'm a grandmother?" she gushed. Yeah, Gloria was definitely excited and Reese couldn't stifle her giggle.

"Yes," Dane said. "He's two years old and his name is Cole."

"Like your father's name?" Gloria questioned, tearing up.

"Ahh, come on, Ma. Not the waterworks," Dane complained. "Yeah, like dad's name."

"Dane and I met three years ago and well, I went home to New York not knowing I was pregnant and I was alone and afraid; I didn't tell your son about the baby," Reese said. Gloria nodded and smiled at her and for some crazy reason, Reese felt at ease.

"I understand, dear," Gloria consoled her, patting the back of Reese's hand with her own. "You had to do what was right for you and your baby. You're here now and that is all that matters."

"Thank you for that," Reese said.

"So, when do I get to meet little Cole?" Gloria asked. She eagerly watched them and Dane laughed and shook his head.

"I'm thinking tomorrow is the best answer here or you'll show up on my doorstep anyway," Dane teased.

"Correct," Gloria confirmed. "I'll be there in time for breakfast and you can introduce me to Cole and I can spend some time getting to know Reese." Dane groaned and rolled his eyes again causing both Reese and Gloria to giggle.

"You have always been so overly dramatic, Dane," his mother teased. "I'll see you both tomorrow," she said, standing to pull them both in for another quick hug. Honestly, the woman was like a tornado and Reese wasn't sure she'd be able to keep up with her.

"Sorry," Dane apologized after his mother was gone. "She can be a bit much."

"No," Reese said. "She's perfect. I wish my mother cared even half as much about me and Cole as yours seems to care about you. It's nice to see that Cole will have at least one grandparent who is excited about being part of his life."

Dane chuckled, "Oh honey, you have no idea. That woman has wanted a grandchild since I can remember. Cole will be the most loved little boy on the planet." Dane seemed to be watching her and she wasn't sure what to do or say next. "How about we go pick up our son and then head back to my condo. It's been a long day for both of us," he said. Reese shyly nodded. She liked the idea of going back to Cole's place and picking up where they left off last night.

It was so late by the time they picked Cole up he had fallen asleep on Toni and Nico's big bed after a full day of playing on the beach. Watching Dane carry her son out to his truck and strapping him into his car seat, had her reliving all those same damn mushing feelings, causing her to dramatically sigh one too many times. If she didn't get herself together she was going to push Dane into giving her something he might not want to give—at least not yet.

Dane pulled into his parking space at his condo and turned off his truck. "I'll carry him up to his room and put him into your bed," he whispered. Reese had to admit she felt a pang of disappointment at Dane's mention of her and Cole sharing a bed again tonight. She nodded and helped him in, making sure Cole was carefully tucked in for the night before setting her sights on changing Dane's mind about where she was going to sleep.

"He's so cute when he's asleep," Dane whispered on their way back to the kitchen. "How about a beer?" he asked. "I'd offer you wine, but I don't keep it here. Most of my guests are male and they'd never stop harassing me if I offered them a nice glass of merlot." Dane crossed his eyes, causing her to giggle. It was nice to hear most of his visitors were men. The idea of being one of his only female guests gave her hope she knew would only lend to disappoint her later.

"Beer is fine," she said. "I'm guessing you don't bring women to your place then. Too messy?" she asked. The sheepish grin he shot her made Reese regret her question. "Sorry," she said. "I tend to overstep my place. I guess I ask a lot of personal questions that aren't really my business. It's the lawyer in me," she admitted. When she was a kid, her grandfather used to tease her she'd make either a really good gossip or a great lawyer. It had basically been decided for her, what she was going to be when she grew up, from the time she was five. Her grandfather and father were both lawyers and the idea of being a gossiping trophy wife like her mother didn't appeal to her.

"No, it's fine," he said. "I'm just not used to anyone caring enough to ask me questions—well, except my old roommate, Jace. Since he moved out, it's been a little quiet around here. To answer your question—no. I don't bring women here because I don't want to get into a messy area where they think I'm available for a relationship." His truth told Reese everything she needed to know.

"I get it," she whispered. "You don't want to lead anyone on. I know the score, Dane and I'm not asking you for forever," she admitted. Reese had never felt so confused. First, Dane said he wanted her to give him a chance to get to know her and Cole and now, he says he doesn't want a messy relationship.

"I think you're missing the point here, honey. You're here, so obviously, something has changed. I can't tell you what that is or why things are different with you, but messy suddenly doesn't seem so scary when you're around," he whispered. Dane pulled her against his body and she liked the way his breath hitched when she wrapped her arms around his shoulders.

"So, you are ready for things to get messy, Dane? Because my entire life is a disaster—messy doesn't even begin to cover it." Reese laughed at her own statement even though there was really nothing funny about it. Her life was a construction zone without the warning signs and flashing lights.

"I like a good fixer-upper," Dane teased. I'm not afraid to get my hands dirty," he said, flexing his fingers into her hips. She was thinking of all the parts of Dane she'd like to make dirty.

"So, when you were talking about taking things slowly, how slow were you planning on going?" she questioned. Suddenly, the idea of Dane wanting to pump the brakes on what was so obviously happening between the two of them only made her want him more.

"I think we should wait to have sex, Reese. If we just jump into bed together now, where does that leave us?" he asked.

"Satisfied," she pouted. Dane chuckled but she found the whole thing a lot less funny.

"Believe me, I want this every bit as much as you do, Reese. I'm just willing to wait to make sure we don't end up living in two separate states again after our night together ends," he said, pushing a strand of her brown hair back out of her eyes.

"Will you at least kiss me good night?" she asked, not hiding her pout. "Please," she added.

"If you promise to behave yourself, yes," he whispered. Dane dipped his head down to gently kiss her mouth but Reese had other ideas. She wrapped her arms around his neck and pulled his body down to hers to deepen the kiss. She loved the feel of his hard body pressed up against her own. It had been so long since she had felt this much desire for any man—three years to be exact and with the same man who currently had her pinned up against his body, kissing her senseless.

"Dane, please," she whimpered, shamelessly rubbing herself against his jean-clad erection. She was willing to beg him if that was what it would take but not having Dane take her back to his room to spend the whole night reminding her just how well they fit together, felt wrong. One way or another, she needed to end up in his bed and she would use all her ploys to get there.

Dane

Reese had her hot little body practically wrapped around his and it took every ounce of his restraint to tell her no—because he wanted to give in to everything they both obviously wanted.

"Dane," Reese whispered against his lips, "I need you." He groaned and took a step back from her effectively untangling her from his body. His cock protested and he had to agree what he was about to do sucked but it was the only way to prove to them both they could work this time.

"We can't," he groaned. "Reese, I want you for more than just one night, baby. We've already talked about this, remember? We're going to take it slow this time; get to know each other for the sake of our son. It won't be fair to Cole if we jump into bed together and don't try to build what we both want."

"I know," Reese moaned, "I remember our conversation, but right now all I can think about is you taking me back to your bed and making me yours again." Dane closed his eyes, not able to erase the mental image of having Reese in his bed or under his body again. He'd give just about anything for it to happen but one of them needed to keep their head and priorities straight.

Dane dipped his head, stealing one more quick kiss from her soft, wet lips. He knew if he took more from her he'd give in to her request and drag her back to his bed. "Good night, Reese," he murmured, causing her to pout.

"You don't sound very happy about telling me goodnight, Dane," she taunted. Reese was right, he was pretty fucking pissed about not taking her back to his room.

"Well, I'm not. But, this is for the best, baby," Dane said. "I'll see you and Cole in the morning, honey," he promised. Dane knew if he didn't turn away from her now, he never would. He walked down the hall to his room and didn't chance a look back. If he saw her needy and breathless watching him walk away from her, he'd turn back around and give her what she wanted—what they both seemed to want.

He shut his door and made his way back to his bathroom, needing a shower. Hell, he needed to get off. He stripped out of his clothes and stepped under the warm spray and groaned while palming his throbbing cock. He leaned back against the cold tiles and thrust his dick into his hand thinking how much he wanted Reese's sweet little lips around his cock, sucking him deep into her hot mouth. Dane closed his eyes allowing visions of her lying across his bed with her legs wrapped around his waist to assault him. He knew jacking off into his hand wasn't ever going to be enough to stay the lust she brought out in him just by being in the same room.

"That's so hot," she moaned. Dane opened his eyes to find Reese standing on the other side of the shower door watching him through the glass. She sent him a pleading look and he couldn't tell if she was asking him to finish getting off or let her join him. He didn't have to figure it out once Reese started stripping. His breath hitched as she slipped her shirt over her head, revealing she wasn't wearing a bra. Dane's mouth watered at the idea of wrapping his lips around her taut nipples. She seemed to read his mind, stripping faster.

"Please don't tell me no," she begged, opening the door to step through the spray of water and into his arms. "I need you too much for you to turn me away now, Dane," she whispered. Reese sealed her lips over his wrapping her hands around his cock and there was no way he could deny her. Every one of his good intentions flew out the window with each stroke of her hands over his unruly dick.

"Yes, honey," he hissed into her mouth. "That feels so fucking good, baby," he praised. Reese gifted him with her sexy smile and kissed her way up his jawline. There was no fucking way he was going to be able to tell her to stop now and from the knowing look in her eyes, she knew exactly what she was doing. If she kept it up things would be over before he even got started.

Dane turned her around so her back was up against the shower wall, switching places with her. Reese protested when he removed her hands from his dick and he had to admit it felt pretty damn wrong to stop her from what she was doing, but he had plans for his sexy little Reese and coming in her hands wasn't a part of them.

"I know, baby but I need to taste you first," he whispered into her ear. Dane pushed her body out of the spray and sank to his knees helping her to balance so she could throw one leg over his shoulder, spreading her open to everything he wanted to do to her.

"Dane, please," she whimpered.

"I'll take good care of you baby," he crooned. He ran two fingers through her slick folds and pumped them inside of her hot core loving the way she bucked and writhed against his hand. He sucked her clit into his mouth and she moaned arching her back against the wall pushing her wet pussy into his mouth. Reese took what she needed from him and he had to admit it was fucking hot to watch.

"Yes Dane, I'm going to come," she shouted. Her whole body tensed and Dane could taste her sweet release as it washed over his tongue. She tasted like honey and was a balm to his battered heart. He knew he'd never get enough of sweet little Reese.

Dane kissed his way up her curves and lifted her against the wall. "I like all of your new curves, baby," he mumbled against her skin. Her body had changed since they were last together. He had a feeling it was due to her giving birth to Cole and he found every one of her sexy curves irresistible.

Reese seemed suddenly shy and he worried that he had said something wrong. "I've gained a little weight since having Cole. My body isn't the same as when we were first together," she whispered.

"You're perfect, baby," Dane said.

Reese's smile was wicked as she wrapped her legs around his waist, all but inviting him to thrust his cock into her ready body. Dane wanted to take his time, but damn, he wanted exactly what she was offering him. Hot, fast sex would get him off. Then, he'd take the rest of the night to make her scream out his name while she was tangled up in his bedsheets.

He thrust his cock into her core and loved the way she moaned in his mouth as he kissed her. She took all of him; everything he had to give her and when she came around his cock, he couldn't hold out any longer. Dane thrust a few more times and lost himself deep inside of Reese.

"Thank you," she whispered against his neck.

Dane chuckled, "You never have to thank me for that, honey."

"No, thank you for today, all of it—waking up with Cole and taking care of him, introducing me to your friends, and taking me on a real date. Thank you for not turning me away tonight and letting me in, Dane. I know you don't easily trust people. I know how much it takes for you to trust that I'm not going anywhere." Dane nodded; not sure he'd be able to answer her. Reese seemed to be able to read every emotion he had running through his mind and wrapped her arms tighter around his neck, pulling him against her body.

"Can I spend the night in your bed?" she asked. Dane nodded against her neck and she giggled. "Well, that's good because I already brought my toothbrush and robe for the morning into your room hoping you'd say yes," she admitted. Dane couldn't help his laugh.

"You're going to be trouble, aren't you?" Dane teased.

"Yep," Reese admitted. "You good with that?" Reese looked up at him and he could see all her hope staring back at him. He already knew his answer and he hated seeing her uncertainty.

"Fuck yeah," he breathed.

Reese let out her pent- up breath and smiled. "Well, how about you take me to your bed then, Dane. I'd love to see what you have planned for the rest of the night." Dane wanted to tell her he was actually planning what he wanted to do with her every night for the rest of her life but he'd get to that. Right now, he just wanted to concentrate on Reese and showing her what she meant to him, the rest would fall into place—he hoped.

K.L. Ramsey

Reese

They spent the rest of the night in his bed and when they finally settled into sleep Reese felt wide awake. "I can't sleep," she whispered against Dane's chest, where she had snuggled in for the night. At first, he didn't make any move or give her any sign he was awake. Finally, he sighed and she smiled.

"What should we do to make you tired, honey?" he questioned, bobbing his eyebrows at her, causing her to giggle.

"Well not that," she teased. "You don't know this about me but sex wakes me up—for hours. Heck, I forgot about that myself," she whispered.

"I feel like we don't really know each other," Dane admitted. "How about we play a little game?" Reese wanted to tease him they had just played a game and she felt she knew him pretty damn well, but it wasn't what he was asking for. Dane wanted to talk and Reese had to admit she wanted to ask him a few questions. He was right they didn't know each other, not really.

"What game?" she asked. Her heart was racing and she was sure he'd be able to feel it beating against his own chest. The thought of getting to know Dane excited her.

"Well, how about we play something like twenty questions," Dane shrugged. He was going for casual, but Reese could tell he was just as nervous about the whole prospect of getting to know each other as she was.

"I'll go first, to show you just how painless this will be. What's your middle name?" he asked. Reese scrunched up her face causing Dane to chuckle. "Oh, come on it can't be that bad," he said.

"It's not the greatest," she admitted. "My mother was trying to be clever so she named me Reese Autumn Summers." Dane whistled and she couldn't help her giggle. Reese always hated her middle name and was planning on dropping it when she married David.

"That's pretty awful," Dane teased. "At least she didn't go full-on seasons and give you the first name winter," he offered. Reese laughed and even found herself relaxing against his body. Dane was right; getting to know each other was painless. She wasn't sure if they were each going to get twenty questions or if they were going to split them. Either way, Reese wanted to make each of her questions count. She thought for a few minutes and then decided to go for an open-ended question that would require more than a yes or no answer. Poor Dane was going to have to put a little effort in and she felt bad he had given her such an easy question.

"Tell me something you have never told anyone else," Reese whispered. Dane smiled at her and for just a minute she thought he wasn't going to give in to her request.

"Hmm," he was so still, she wondered if she should recant her question and ask a simpler one to start. "Well, when I was in fifth grade," Dane started, "I was asked to play a make out game, 'Seven Minutes in Heaven'," he said. Honestly, she had only heard of the game but was never allowed to attend parties with friends. She was never asked to play the game.

"I've heard of it," she said.

Dane nodded and continued, "Well, Jackie Ritter asked me to go into the closet with her and I was pretty sure I was going to throw up, I was so excited. It was the first time I had ever been alone with a girl, let alone kiss one. At first, I told her no and the other kids taunted me and called me a chicken. Finally, I couldn't take any more of the clucking and taunting so I grabbed her hand and pulled her into the closet, taking her up on her offer."

"So, you got your first kiss?" Reese asked. It was crazy to think of Dane as ever being inexperienced. He seemed so sure of himself now; picturing him as a shy little boy almost seemed foreign to her.

"Well, kind of," he admitted. "It was all an elaborate joke my classmates were playing on me. You see, I was what you might call a nerd back when I was a kid. I was skinny and wore thick glasses and even had braces. The other kids loved to pick on me and that party was no exception. Jackie was in the closet with me because the other kids put her up to it," Dane said. A part of Reese's heart ached for the little boy he used to be and she wrapped her arms tighter around him.

"Oh Dane, that's horrible," she whispered. "Kids can be so cruel."

"I got the last laugh though," he admitted. Reese looked up to find him smiling and she was a little more hopeful his story would have a happy ending. "When she admitted she was only in the closet with me because the other kids put her up to it I threw the door open giving the whole class a show. I pulled Jackie into my arms and kissed her like I had seen grown-ups do in the movies. When I finished kissing her I strutted out of the closet and right out of the house to throw up in the host's front bushes." Reese full-on belly laughed.

"No," she gasped.

"Yep and do you know what those little fuckers talked about Monday morning when we all got back to school?" Reese shook her head, almost too afraid to guess. "All they could talk about was the fact that I threw up after I kissed Jackie Ritter. There were rumors flying around she gave me cooties and we were both labeled as social pariahs." Dane shook his head almost as if he still couldn't believe it even after all these years.

"Well, I don't feel bad for Jackie. She did it to herself, but you poor thing," she soothed.

"Naw—don't feel too bad for Jackie. She grew up just fine. We even dated senior year, but she married the high school quarterback and from what I hear they are still together and have a few kids." Dane kissed the top of her head. "My turn again," he whispered.

"Yeah," she said. Reese sighed and waited him out and from the time it was taking him to come up with his next question she started to worry just how bad it was going to be.

"Why did you pick me, you know—our first night together?" Dane asked. "You could have had your pick of guys that night, but you asked me to give you what you needed." Reese thought back to that night but she already knew the answer. From the moment she saw him she knew he wouldn't hurt her. Dane seemed safe—a little corny and a whole lot arrogant but safe. She knew he would give her what she needed and not take advantage of her or demand more.

"You were pretty hard to ignore." Reese shrugged. "And well, you have a mirror," she teased. Dane seemed to realize she wasn't giving him her full answer and the look of disappointment he shot her was one that rivaled her own when Cole had done something wrong.

"Fine," she said. "I chose you because I knew you wouldn't hurt me. You seemed like a nice guy despite you're really cheesy pick-up lines and I somehow knew you wouldn't take advantage of me—well, any more than I was asking you to."

Dane kissed her forehead and she felt it was the sweetest gesture. "Thank you, honey," he whispered. "I would never hurt you," he agreed.

"I know Dane, and I feel the same way about you," she whispered. She wanted to spill her guts and tell him just how she felt about him, but she worried admitting her feelings to him would be a mistake. Reese wasn't sure she would be able to handle his rejection.

"I'm not sure if you know just how I feel about you, honey," he growled. "I'm pretty sure this might scare the shit out of you—hell, I know it does me but I'm falling for you, Reese."

She wasn't sure what to say, or even if she should say anything. "How can you say that, Dane? We've essentially only known each other for a matter of days." Reese knew better than to get her hopes up when it came to a promise made by a man. She heard those same promises from David and he broke every one of them. Telling Dane she was feeling the same way about him could prove dangerous to her heart but if she never took the leap again how would she find real happiness? Didn't she owe it to both herself and Cole to find some form of joy because she wasn't happy living in New York being a single mother? Her son was her life and she wouldn't change it for the world, but she was lonely and her memories of her and Dane's night together only stretched so far on those long nights spent alone in her bed.

Dane shrugged, "I can't explain any of this," he groaned as if he was just as frustrated with his feelings as she was. "All I can tell you is after I walked away from you three years ago; I spent almost a year trying to get you out of my head."

"Wow," she whispered. "I'm not sure if I should be flattered or what. But, if we are being honest here, I felt the same way, Dane. I haven't been with anyone else since you," she admitted. Dane's body stilled under her and she swore even his breathing stopped.

"You mean to say you haven't had sex since we were together three years ago?" he questioned and she felt like a complete freak for admitting the truth.

"Yeah," she admitted. "I was a little busy growing a human and dealing with my ex and my father's disapproval. When Cole was born, I eventually ventured out on a date or two, but once I admitted I had a baby waiting at home for me the guy I was with usually bolted."

"Well, I can't say I'm upset they did, honey. Otherwise, you would have never come to me and I wouldn't know Cole. But they were all idiots. Fuck, I was an idiot for walking away from you." Hearing Dane admit that to her, melted her defenses some.

"But you did walk away, Dane. We both knew what we were getting into. I was the one who asked you for one night—you were just giving me what I wanted at the time," Reese admitted.

"I know but I wish I would have been in a different place emotionally then. When my father died, I had to be the strong one for my mother. You know, the man of the house, but I was just a kid still. I think losing him as a teen influenced the way I chose to live my life," he said. Reese nodded but didn't say anything. She wanted to let him get the rest out. "I became a lifeguard with my friend Jace because it seemed like a fun job. And it was for a while. I became the cliché party boy, always looking for a good time and an easy hook-up. As I got older I started thinking about what I wanted my future to look like and the night I met you, a part of me thought I found what I was looking for. But, when you told me you loved me and then called me your ex's name—well, it pissed me off. So, I did what I usually do and bolted. Jace hounded me to find more for myself, and I didn't have the heart to tell him I had and I just walked out of your life like a fool."

Reese couldn't take any more of his confessions, not without telling him a few of her own. "I'm falling for you too, Dane," Reese admitted. Not saying it felt like a lie and she was done being too afraid to admit what she wanted or how she was feeling.

"Thank fuck, baby," Dane breathed and wrapped his arms tighter around her body. "I thought I was alone in all of this."

"No," she breathed. "But where do we go from here? You live here and I live in New York." She hated thinking of not living in her favorite city, but honestly, there was nothing waiting there for her anymore. "Although, I'm pretty sure I don't have a job to go back to and I know for a fact my father will make it damn near impossible to find another job in the city." She could feel the tension rolling off Dane's body and she knew talking about her father pissed him off. Reese loved the way he felt so protective of her, but she was used to taking care of herself. Having someone else in her corner was going to take some getting used to.

"How about we just take this—well, whatever this is—one day at a time? I won't make you any promises I can't keep and you do the same. I think we can find some common ground if we just give this half a chance, baby," Dane whispered and kissed the top of her head. Reese nodded, hoping like hell he was right because losing him now would be more than she could handle.

Dane

Dane woke to find Cole standing at the side of the bed, staring at him, with a big goofy grin on his little face. "Pancakes," the toddler shouted and smiled even bigger. Dane couldn't help but smile back at him. His son sure loved his pancakes and who could blame the kid. He felt the same way about Cole's breakfast choice and while he wouldn't mind having some pancakes with his son, he was going to have to head to work soon. He stretched and pulled Cole into bed with them loving the way he snuggled in between him and Reese. Having both of them in his bed felt right like they were a real family and hadn't spent the first two years of Cole's life in two separate states.

Reese seemed dead to the world and Dane wondered if she had slept much these past two years since having Cole. He felt a pang of remorse for not being there for the two of them and he wondered if she would have given him the chance if he would have wanted to be a part of Cole's life. He really didn't have his shit together, but a part of him wanted to believe he would have done the right thing by both of them. Now, there was no question in Dane's mind—he wanted them both.

He scooped up Cole and headed to the living room, to find a cartoon for the toddler to watch just as someone started pounding on the front door. He knew to be cautious given the fact Reese still had someone who possibly wanted to hurt her or Cole, but who would even know they were there with him?

Dane looked out the peephole to see a voluptuous blonde standing on the other side of the door and from the looks of her, she had been crying. He sighed, knowing the chances of two women showing up on his doorstep claiming to have had his baby, was slim to none. He was usually careful but it was always a possibility. Dane pulled the door open and from the way the curvy blonde looked him up and down and then smiled, this was the first time they had met. Most women he fell into bed with didn't treat him so friendly after he left their beds.

"Can I help you?" Dane asked. Honestly, the last thing he needed now was to deal with unwanted flirting. Cole had run back to the bedroom to wake up Reese. She sauntered out into the living room wiping sleep from her eyes wearing just his t-shirt and she looked good enough to eat.

"Reese?" the woman cried, shoving past Dane and into his condo to pull Reese into her arms. Reese's body went rigid and from her sour expression, she was a lot less happy about their reunion.

"Amber, what the hell are you doing here?" Reese questioned. Yeah, she was not happy about their visitor. Reese pulled away from the woman's embrace and took a step back from her, effectively giving herself some breathing room.

"I have awful news," the woman pouted and Reese rolled her eyes.

"Is it worse than you running away with my fiancé on the day of my wedding? Or maybe it's worse than my own best friend stabbing me in the back and turning all of my friends against me?" Reese crossed her arms over her body and Dane couldn't take the sullen look she shot him. He could tell Reese hated rehashing her painful past in front of him, but there was no way he was leaving her alone with their company. He shut his front door and scooped up Cole, causing him to giggle.

"Why are you here exactly, Amber?" Reese asked again.

"Is this your little guy?" Amber asked. "I'm assuming you are her big guy too?" She crossed the small room with her hand extended to Dane and introduced herself. "I'm Amber Prince," she purred and Dane made no move to take her extended hand. Reese shot him a smile from behind Amber's back and he winked at her causing her to bark out her laugh.

"I think you need to answer Reese's question, Amber," Dane said.

Amber lowered her hand and turned back to face Reese. As soon as she did, the waterworks started again and Reese shook her head. "Try to keep it together, Amber. I'll ask you this one last time, why are you here? You have thirty seconds to answer me and then I'll have Dane throw you out."

Amber sighed and quickly turned off the theatrics, seeing that they would have no effect on Reese. "Fine, I'm here to let you know David is dead," she dryly said. Amber wasted no fanfare spilling the news. It was as if she was talking about someone neither of them knew, let alone someone who they both slept with.

"What?" Reese asked. Dane crossed the room and wrapped his arm around Reese, pulling her into his side. "How?"

"The police aren't really sure about how but that's partially why I'm here. You really need to come back to New York; they have some questions they'd like to ask you." Amber almost sounded gleeful as she gave Reese the news.

"Am I a suspect?" Reese questioned.

Amber shrugged, "I guess we all are. They just have a few questions about where you were two nights ago. You know, they are just crossing all their t's and dotting all their I's," Amber said.

"I was here two nights ago. It was the night I got into town," Reese all but whispered.

"Well, then you should just head on up to the city and give them your alibi," Amber offered. They'll let you go, I'm guessing. But, I'm no lawyer," she sassed.

"So it happened two nights ago?" Reese asked.

"Yes," Amber said. "It was horrible. I found him in our apartment that night after my spin class. Honestly, you should know we were splitting up. I was just living there until I could find something that suited my needs." Amber seemed to be a spoiled rich girl and the coldness Dane heard in Amber's tone made him wonder how Reese could be best friends with the stone-cold bitch.

"How did you know where to find Reese?" Dane asked. Nothing seemed to be adding up and he was trying to figure out why Amber would make the trip all the way down to the island when she could have easily called to give Reese the bad news.

Amber plastered a smile on her face and Dane was sure any answer she was about to give him would be a lie. "Her father has a private investigator tailing her to make sure she is safe." Amber quickly amended. Dane just bet her father's primary objective was to keep her safe.

"So my father told you where to find me?" Reese seemed panicked and Dane knew she was thinking about taking Cole and running. What Reese didn't realize was she didn't have to run this time. He'd keep both of them safe.

"Yep," Amber slid down onto the sofa. "Do you have any coffee? It's been a long trip," Amber said, making herself right at home. Reese shot Dane a pleading look and he knew if they let Amber get comfortable, she wasn't going to be going anywhere anytime soon. Reese would want to figure out her next step and honestly, he was thinking the same thing.

"How about you tell us exactly what you are doing here, Amber and then I'll give you directions to the nearest coffee shop?" Dane offered. Amber clutched her chest and gasped as if Dane had physically hurt her. She seemed like a real drama queen and Dane wondered how Reese could ever be friends with a woman like her.

"Well, I see the rumor about people in the south having better manners is a falsehood," Amber said. "I don't understand why you seem so put off I'm here. I came to tell one of my oldest friends that her ex-fiancée is dead. I thought I already went over that part," she grouched. Dane wasn't sure why but the woman grated on his last nerve and her just showing up here had to be more than just a coincidence. Amber wanted something but from whom and what, he had no idea.

"And Reese's father told you where to find her and what asked you to come down personally and deliver the news?" Dane questioned.

"Well, yes. Actually, I volunteered my services when Robert explained the pickle he was in. He wanted to make sure Reese knew about David, but he said you two weren't exactly on speaking terms as of late," Amber said, looking Reese up and down as if she was judging her and finding her wanting.

"No," Reese all but whispered. "We are not on speaking terms and haven't been since my failed attempt at walking down the aisle. But, you made sure to keep David company while the rest of my so-called friends told me about how they all slept with my fiancé."

Amber laughed and stood. "You know, Reese, I'm starting to think you're not upset about David's death. Maybe the detective handling his case would be interested to know how calmly you are taking the news." Dane growled and stepped in front of Reese as if trying to block Amber's nasty threats with his body. Amber giggled again and Reese side-stepped him to face her old friend.

"I think it's time for you to go, Amber. I won't pretend to be upset about David. I really don't feel anything at all towards him or you, for that matter. I lost interest in both of you the day you stabbed me in the back and ran away with my fiancé. I hope you get everything you deserve, Amber, and so much more," Reese spat. Amber collected her jacket and bag to find her way out of his condo and Dane was happy to see her go. Amber slammed the door behind her, causing Cole to whimper. Dane held his son against his chest trying to calm him. He fucking hated that he allowed someone like Amber around Cole but she really left him no choice.

"She seems great," he teased but judging from the look Reese shot him, she wasn't in a teasing mood.

"I can't believe I was ever friends with her or any of them," she said.

"What are we going to do next?" Dane questioned. He didn't want to leave any doubt he and Reese were a team.

"I think Cole and I need to find a safe place to go. I can't stay here knowing my father has found me. It won't be long before he sends someone besides Amber to find us and I can't let it happen. I think he was sending me another message by having Amber come here. My father wants to let me know he found us," Reese said. She had already started picking up Cole's toys and he knew she was packing their stuff to move on. What she didn't realize was he was going to be going with them. They were a team now—she was his, even if she didn't remember the promise she made him.

"Where are we going to go?" Dane asked.

"Dane, you don't need to get caught up in my mess," she whispered. "I appreciate the offer though." Dane looked down to where Cole rested his head against his chest, calmly sucking his thumb and smiled.

"I'm already caught up in this mess, honey. You and Cole are mine and I'm not letting you just walk out of my life again. I've already told you how I feel about wanting my shot with you—both of you. That hasn't changed for me just because your past is a little messy." Dane crossed the room to where Reese was still picking up Cole's things and stopped her, pulling her into his arms.

"Please just let me figure this all out, Dane," Reese sobbed. She leaned in against him and they sandwiched Cole's little body between the two of them. It felt perfect having them both in his arms.

"There is nothing to figure out, baby. This right here is what is important. The three of us are a family now and I won't let either of you go," he whispered. "We can figure out the rest together." Reese nodded and Dane felt himself exhale.

"I guess we need to head up to New York then," she whispered. "I need to speak with the detective who is handling David's case. If my hunch is correct, his death has something to do with the threatening letters I've been getting." Dane knew Reese was probably right but he hated walking back into the lion's den, so to speak. If he had his way they would be running the opposite direction of New York but he knew Reese wouldn't back down. She seemed like someone who would never back down from a challenge; it was one of the many things he liked about her. Ready or not, they were heading to New York, but this time he would be by Reese's side and no one would touch her or his son.

K.L. Ramsey

Reese

They landed in Laguardia Airport the next day and Reese had to admit she was regretting her decision to go back to New York. Bringing both Dane and Cole with her might be dragging them both into danger and it was the last thing she wanted. She really appreciated that Dane wanted to be with her and Cole, hell—she wasn't sure how she would have gotten through the last twenty-four hours without him.

After Dane all but kicked Amber out of his condo he called his mother and quickly explained everything to her and she seemed to understand that her meeting Cole for the first time was going to have to be postponed. Reese hated disappointing Gloria but she said that she understood. Dane promised that as soon as everything died down and they could safely plan a visit home he would.

Dane got off the phone with his mom and helped her pack and they left the island. He arranged for them to stay at a hotel close to the airport, knowing his condo might be compromised. Dane knew the manager of the hotel and he gave orders that no one was to know they were there. She loved the way he wanted to protect both Cole and her. She didn't miss the bond forming between Dane and Cole and every time she saw them together her heart melted a little. It was everything she had wanted over the last three years but wouldn't let her heart hope for.

Reese also noted the way Dane was constantly touching her and kissing her and her overactive libido was out of control. After not being with a man for so long, Dane had her body all revved up and ready for more.

"We can't stay at my apartment," she said. Dane was pulling their bags down from the overhead compartment as she tried to soothe Cole. Her son wasn't really a fan of flying and he let all of the poor passengers have an earful of his complaining for most of the flight to New York.

"I already worked all of it out," Dane said. He took Cole from her and the toddler instantly calmed, making her grimace. Dane laughed and she couldn't help her smile.

"He's certainly taken to you," she whispered. Reese was amazed that in just a few short days the three of them went from being virtual strangers to looking like a happy little family. She just worried it was all just smoke and mirrors and once she and Cole were out of danger, their mirage would disappear.

"I'm not sure where you just went to, honey but judging from the look on your face I won't like it," Dane said. "I've made arrangements for us to stay at Toni's place. Her family has an apartment in the city and she said we can stay there for as long as we need to. Plus, there is great security already in place and she has called ahead to put some extra men on the job. I'm not taking any chances with you, Reese—with either of you," he whispered and kissed the top of Cole's head.

Dane had thought of everything down to having a car waiting for them ready to whisk them off to Toni's apartment. It wasn't far from her own, just five blocks away. Dane must have felt like a fish out of water; her city was quite a culture shock from his island paradise but he didn't show it. Reese looked over her shoulder at every turn as if waiting for trouble to catch up with them. She didn't feel like she even took a breath until they were safe in Toni's spacious apartment.

They got Cole settled and he was asleep in no time. Reese felt lost not knowing what to do next and it was foreign to her. She was always so in control but since finding out David had been killed, she wasn't feeling very self-assured. She loved the way Dane seemed to realize how lost she was feeling and tried to take care of her and Cole.

Dane found her in the bathroom waiting for the shower to heat up and wrapped his arms around her, watching her in the mirror. "I have scheduled a meeting with the detective in charge of David's case," Dane admitted. "I hope it is alright with you. They wanted us to come down to the station."

Reese smiled at his reflection, "Thanks," she said. "I have to admit this whole thing with David has thrown me for a loop. I feel as though I'm walking through a dream ever since Amber landed on your doorstep." Dane's smile disappeared and she worried she said something wrong.

"Do you still have feelings for him?" Dane asked. She almost wanted to laugh at his question, but then she saw he was serious and she instantly regretted that he was so unsure of how she felt.

Reese turned to face Dane, wrapping her arms around his neck, "I don't have feelings for David," she admitted. "I haven't for a long time, well—three years to be exact. Being with you changed things for me in more ways than you'll ever know, Dane." She went up on her tiptoes to gently kiss his lips.

"Well, having my kid must have really changed your life," he teased.

Reese giggled, "Sure, but I'm not really talking about the fact you gave me the best gift anyone has ever given me. You really ruined me for all other guys. I think it's why I've had such a tough time jumping back into the whole dating pool." She knew she was giving away her hand, but she didn't care. Reese knew she was strong enough to handle just about anything now, including Dane's rejection.

"What are we doing here, Dane?" she whispered. Reese held her breath, sorry she just blurted out her question but she wanted to know his answer more than anything.

"You mean this thing between us?" he questioned.

"Yeah," she sighed.

"I thought I was clear the other night, baby. I'm falling in love with you," he whispered back. Reese's breath hitched.

"You said you were falling for me but there was no mention of the 'L' word. I would definitely remember if there had been any reference to that word." She felt as though her heart was going to beat right out of her chest but she couldn't help it.

"How would you feel about us introducing that word into this whole scenario?" Dane waited her out while she tried to get herself back under control. He could already read her so well.

Reese took a deep breath and decided to just jump. "I think I'm already past introducing it, Dane." God, why was this so hard? Reese wanted to hide but Dane wasn't having it. He watched her and waited for her to finish.

"Fine," she yelled. "I'm in love with you. Does that make you happy?" she spat.

"Well, I'd be a whole lot happier about your declaration if you didn't seem so angry about admitting it, baby. I'm in love with you too," he growled. Reese couldn't help her giggle. The whole conversation sounded more like their first fight and not two people telling each other they loved the other for the very first time.

"You do?" she asked. Reese covered her mouth with her shaking hand and she wasn't sure what to do or say next. She had told David she loved him and maybe she meant it at the time, but with Dane, things felt so different. Her relationship with David felt more mechanical, predictable but everything with Dane felt unruly, like being caught in the eye of a storm and not being able to break free from the destruction in its path. Dane was her storm and her anchor all rolled up in one sexy as sin package.

"I do," he answered. "Does it scare you?" he asked.

Reese shook her head, "No," she lied. Honestly, she had never been more terrified of anything in her life. She faced down being left at the altar, becoming a single mother and facing her father's scrutiny day in and day out and none of those things scared her like her feelings for Dane did.

"Liar," he teased. When Dane smiled at her the way he was she felt as though she couldn't catch her breath.

"So, tomorrow we go in to talk to the police, then what?" she questioned. She hoped Dane wouldn't catch on to her changing the subject, but she wasn't that lucky.

"Okay honey, I'll let you hide for a little while longer. But, sooner or later you and I will have to figure out just what we are doing here. Feelings aside, we have a son involved and I won't fuck up his life, Reese. Cole is too important; you both are." Reese nodded, hoping her non-verbal agreement would be enough. She didn't want to discuss feelings anymore tonight. She needed a plan and a damn good one at that. It would be the only way to keep Cole safe because being back in New York had her panicking. She worried they were walking right back into danger and Reese hated feeling so helpless.

"Tomorrow we talk to the police and then I say we pay your dad a little visit. It's about time he meets Cole's father. Hell, he's already weighed and measured me; don't you think he should properly meet me?" Dane waited for her answer and honestly, she didn't have one. On the one hand, she knew he was right and she liked facing her enemy head-on. But, seeing her father again was something she dreaded. She hadn't left things on good terms with him. The last time she had a full conversation with her dad she threatened to go after him and his company if he dared fire her for getting pregnant. Reese really hadn't spoken much to him since Cole was born and she wanted to keep things that way between the two of them.

"I don't know if it's such a good idea," she stuttered. "My father is not a nice man, Dane." Not nice was an understatement. He was a downright nasty human being lacking any capacity for kindness or compassion.

"So I've gathered, baby. We can't just cower here, waiting for him to make his next move. If he is the person who's trying to hurt my son, I think it's time I let him know he'll have to come through me now. Maybe it will help deter him coming after you and Cole," Dane said.

Reese trusted Dane and if he thought it was a good idea to go visit her father, it's what they would do. She knew he'd be by her side and it was all of the reassurances she needed. She wrapped her arms around his neck and pulled him down to gently brush her lips over his. It had been a long day but her tired body hummed to life with every kiss and the way he touched her, holding her against his body.

"Alright," she conceded. "We will do this your way," she said.

"Thank you for that, baby," he said, kissing his way into her mouth. Dane took her to the edge of sanity every time he kissed her. It was as though he was trying to tell her everything he was feeling just by kissing and touching her. And every time, he left her wanting more from him, craving everything he was promising her and everything he needed from her in return.

K.L. Ramsey

Dane

The next morning they woke up and had breakfast just as they had the past handful of mornings back on the island. This morning they were going to have to go down to the police department and deal with the mess David's death had left in its wake. Dane hated that Reese was mixed up in the whole ordeal but once she submitted her alibi, they should be over their first hurdle. He had to admit the second blockade in their way, Reese's dad, might not prove to be so easy.

He wasn't afraid to meet Robert Summers, but he had to admit he already didn't care for him. If the fear in Reese's eyes was any indication, the man was an asshole who enjoyed terrorizing his own flesh and blood. His plan was simple, meet Reese's dad and let him know if he was coming for Cole, he'd have to deal with him now. There was no way he'd let anyone harm his son or Reese. She was his now too, whether she knew it or not.

They got down to her father's building a little after lunchtime and his assistant had the nerve to make the three of them wait in the lobby while shooting Reese daggers over her desk. Dane hated that everyone in the office looked at Reese as if they were judging her. He didn't give a fuck what they thought about him but she wasn't worthy of their scrutiny.

"Is it always like this?" Dane whispered. He cradled Cole's sleeping form against his body. She smiled at him, leaning in to kiss Cole's head.

"Just since this little guy came into the world. Honestly, I don't even notice it anymore. At first, the snide remarks, whispers, and looks all wore me down. I thought about quitting more times than I'd like to admit. But, if I quit, he'd win." Reese looked back over to where her father's personal assistant was still mean-mugging her and rolled her eyes. "They would all win, and I wouldn't allow that," she said a little louder and with more heat.

The humming sound of disapproval let them know Robert's assistant had heard Reese's comment and wasn't happy about having the tables turned back on her. She pretended to busy herself with some filing and paperwork, occasionally glancing over to make sure they were still in place, sitting on the very uncomfortable bench awaiting the arrival of Reese's father.

After about a half an hour, Reese stood and quietly whispered something to the snooty assistant that had her jumping up and going into her boss's office. Reese stifled her giggle, watching the woman get so flustered and returned to the bench to take her seat next to Dane.

"What did you just say to her?" he questioned.

Reese giggled, covering her mouth with her hand as if trying to muffle the sound. "Well, I reminded Stephanie we were once friends and I knew she was sleeping with my father—that's how she got to be his personal assistant after only working here for six months. That is also the reason why Stephanie and I are no longer friends," she whispered.

Dane threw back his head and laughed. Cole stirred in his arms and for a minute, he worried he might have woken the toddler. He didn't want him to be awake for the part of the day where Dane threatened his grandfather. He didn't want his son to ever see that side of him. But, he would make sure that before they left Robert Summer's office, Reese's dad would receive the message that they were his.

Cole squirmed and then settled into Dane's arms, falling back to sleep. He breathed a sigh of relief and Reese giggled beside him again. "That was a close call," she whispered.

"Yeah," he agreed. "I'm assuming Stephanie is letting your dad know we will be seeing him now?"

"Unless she wants me filling in her husband that she has been and probably still is sleeping with her boss," she whispered with a little more heat.

Dane softly whistled. "Remind me never to get on your bad side, honey," he teased. The office door swung open and Stephanie exited first, not even bothering to look in their direction. The man Dane assumed was Reese's father sauntered out into the waiting area and greeted them both with a scowl. Robert Summers was impeccably dressed and his disposition told Dane that not too many people chose to challenge him—well, until now.

"This better be necessary, Reese. I have a good deal on my plate today, with David's arrangements and investigation. I assume that is why you are back in the city?" he questioned. Dane didn't like the way Reese shivered next to him and he reached for her hand, trying to give her some comfort. Her father didn't show any warmth or caring towards her or Cole and Dane's heart broke for the childhood Reese must have endured. His parents were always so loving and caring. He remembered wishing they would care a little less about what he was doing. Seeing who Reese had to grow up with made Dane suddenly thankful for every time his mother snooped through his room.

"I am here to give my statement and I thought I would swing by to clean out my office and say goodbye," she said.

"Your office has already been cleaned out. When you didn't show up to work a few days in a row, I assumed you weren't coming back. I took the liberty of having your belongings boxed and delivered to your apartment." Her father's tone showed no concern or even curiosity as to why his daughter just stopped showing up for work.

"Did you even know where Reese was or what she was going through? Did you care?" Dane asked. He was done with standing quietly by while Reese handled her father.

"I'm sorry, who are you?" Robert Summers looked him up and down, his squinting eyes resting on Dane's face and he could tell the man knew exactly who he was.

"I'm your grandson's father. My name is Dane Knight," he said, trying to sound as menacing as possible.

"Yes, you are the caveman who picked my daughter up in a bar and got her pregnant. Well, I'd say it was nice to meet you, but it's not," he spat. Dane handed Cole to Reese and she sent him a pleading look not to do anything rash. He smiled and winked at her, letting her know he had this.

"I'm not just your daughter's one night stand, Mr. Summers. I'm the man who loves her and will spend the rest of my life trying to make her happy," Dane said. He took a few steps in the older man's direction and he saw a hint of panic behind his eyes. He liked knowing he had that power over Reese's father, to make him a little uncomfortable. It was just where Dane wanted him.

"Sure, that's what they all say. Once he drains your bank accounts he'll take off leaving you all alone again. That's what you are, Reese—alone." Dane hated that her father was addressing her and not him. It was easier for her father to attack Reese then to have to deal with his threat, but he wasn't about to let him continue.

Dane stepped in Robert's sightline of Reese, blocking her from his view. "From now on, Mr. Summers," Dane spat, "you'll deal directly with me. You have a problem with Reese, you call me. Got it?" he questioned. At first, Dane wasn't sure he was going to get a response. Finally, Reese's father nodded and turned to walk back into his office.

He grabbed his door as if he was going to slam it shut and turned to face them once more. "Please tell my daughter she's fired then," he barked, slamming the door between them. Cole woke and cried, frightened from the loud noise. The only thing Dane wanted to do was march into his office and pound the man who treated Reese so coldly, but she stopped him before he even took one step towards the closed office door.

"He's not worth it, Dane," she whispered, putting her hand on his shoulder as if to hold him back.

"I know. But, I just want to punch him—just once," he admitted.

Reese laughed. "Yeah, well get in line," she said. "I've wanted to punch him my whole life but it won't do either of us any good. We'd be sitting in a jail cell and then who would take care of Cole?" Dane turned back to take the crying toddler from her arms and he instantly calmed. She smirked up at Dane and he couldn't help his own smile. Reese was right, his family was too important to take out his frustrations on her father's face. Dane was just happy she was free of having to show up to work in the same office as her awful father, day in and day out.

"Let's grab a quick lunch and then head down to the station so you can give your statement," he offered. Reese nodded and stopped, pulling out her phone from her bag. She typed out what Dane assumed to be a text and smiled when she hit send. Judging from the devilish grin she wore Reese had just done something she shouldn't have. She walked over to Stephanie's desk and held up her phone showing the woman her screen.

"Just an FYI, Steph," she mock whispered. "I just sent your husband and my mother the pictures you shared with me. You know the ones from when you and my dad spent the weekend in Aspen. The ones of the two of you half-naked," Reese made a face like she was going to puke. Stephanie, on the other hand, couldn't seem to find her voice. "Aww, honey. I'm sure they will both find the whole text as funny as I did. If not, I know of a few good divorce lawyers who might be willing to help you out." Reese pocketed her phone and turned to take Dane's arm with her shaking hand.

"You are so fucking awesome," Dane whispered, kissing her forehead.

"I'm just sick of taking people's shit, Dane. I think they forgot who I am and it's time I started reminding people. Stephanie was just the first stop on my tour. I have dirt on everyone in this office and before the week is done, I'll make sure it spreads like wildfire." Dane wasn't sure if he was impressed or scared to death but he knew for sure he was a whole lot turned on. Reese was a strong, capable, kick-ass woman and he'd never get tired of watching her in action. His woman was a warrior.

K.L. Ramsey

Reese

They spent a few hours exploring New York and watching Dane's wonder at every nuance she found to be part of her mundane routine was exhilarating. Four o'clock rolled by and they had to meet with the detective who had been assigned to David's case. She knew they wouldn't let Dane be in the room with her while they questioned her and she was grateful. Reese knew they would ask personal questions about her and David's relationship and she didn't want Dane to have to hear every sorted detail. He already knew too much about how she was humiliated and dumped on her wedding day. Hell, he saw what it did to her firsthand. Reese handed Cole to Dane knowing he would keep their son safe and busy while she answered the questions.

"I'll be right here waiting for you when you're done," he promised. She had to admit, Dane being with her gave her the courage to do all the things she ran from when she was alone. She faced down her father with his help and now, she was going to make sure everyone knew what a slimeball her ex-fiancé was.

Reese followed the police officer back to a small room and almost laughed at the fact that it looked just like all the interrogation rooms on those cop shows—the ones with the two-way mirrors. It was always funny that the criminals were surprised that they were being watched behind what looked like a mirror. Even though she was a lawyer and had spent countless hours in rooms just like this one, she always found the whole scene humorous.

"Detective Reyes will be with you in a moment, Ms. Summers," the officer said. Reese nodded and sat down at the table. It felt like an eternity before a stout man in a really bad brown suit walked into the small room, shutting the door behind him. She knew she should be taking this whole thing more seriously but the stern expression he wore only made her want to giggle.

"Ms. Summers, I'm detective Reyes," he grumbled, sitting in the chair across from her. "Thank you for coming in today."

"Actually detective, I had to travel up from where I've been living with my son's father." Reese knew she was jumping the gun a bit but she wanted to get right to it. The grumpy looking police detective had already wasted most of her evening by making her wait for him.

"When exactly did you move in with your boyfriend?" he questioned. She smiled at his use of the word boyfriend. Was that who Dane was to her now? He felt like so much more than just a boyfriend. He was her son's father and the man she was in love with but they hadn't really defined what they were to each other yet.

"I got to the island five days ago but I didn't go directly to my boyfriend's," she said, not hiding her smile. "Sorry, it's just all so new to me; you know the whole boyfriend thing? I mean, if we are calling a spade a spade here, he's really a guy I had a one night stand with three years ago. And well, my son's father—you know from the one nightstand. I mean, sure we are together now and Lord help me, I've fallen in love with him but who knows—you know?" Reese looked across the table at the detective who sat with his mouth gaped open, just staring back at her.

"Um, I'm not sure if I'm the right person to talk to about your personal relationship, Ms. Summers." The poor guy seemed to be a little flustered which was evident from his bright red face.

"Would you like some water, detective? You look a little uncomfortable. Are you feeling alright?" she asked. He waved her off when she started fussing over him, telling her that he didn't need any water.

"Alright then, do you have any questions for me?" she asked.

"Ms. Summers, I've only asked you the one question. I have a few more if you don't mind," he grumbled.

"Sure, no problem. Although, I'm sure my, um—boyfriend will be able to collaborate with my alibi. I'm a lawyer, but you wouldn't mind me calling my personal lawyer if your questions are too invasive, right?" Reese waited him out knowing her rights.

"Absolutely Ms. Summers. Would you like to call your lawyer in yet?" he asked. She smiled across the table and shook her head.

"No, so far, so good." She watched as the detective opened the folder he carried into the interrogation room to study the papers inside.

"It says here you and the victim were engaged to be married." Detective Reyes looked up at her and smiled. "Care to elaborate?"

"I'm not sure what you are looking for but yes, we were engaged. In fact, we had a wedding he didn't show up for since he was busy at the time." Reese pretended to pick a speck of lint from her jacket, going for nonchalant. This was all a game and she just needed to keep her head on straight and her temper in check.

"What was he busy doing at the time of your wedding?" he asked.

Reese laughed, "Well, at that exact time, he was busy doing my Maid of Honor, Amber Prince." Her tone sounded a little more put off than she hoped it would. She was over David cheating on her, but being asked questions, dredging up the past was like pouring salt on her wounds.

"I bet that made you angry," Detective Reyes baited her.

"Sure," she said, waving her hand as if waving off a pesky fly. "At the time, three years ago it pissed me off. But, it was a long time ago. David was never faithful to me. I found out he cheated with every woman who was a part of my wedding and then ran away with Amber Prince. I understand that they were still living together at the time of his death."

"And you know this how?" the detective asked.

Reese sighed, growing tired of this game. "I know this because Amber showed up to the condo, where I was staying with Dane, to tell me David was killed."

"Ms. Prince paid you a visit?" he questioned.

"Yes, why?" she asked.

"We've been trying to contact her for days now. After she reported your ex's murder she came into the station to answer a few questions. We told her not to leave the city but we haven't been able to locate her since," he admitted. Reese was trying to follow along, not sure if she was reading more into the situation than was there.

"Are you saying Amber is a suspect in the case?" she asked. Detective Reyes pressed his lips together as if he had already said too much, but Reese could tell she was dead on with her assumption.

"When was the last time you saw Ms. Prince?" he asked.

"Two days ago. She came to Dane's condo on the island, to tell me David was dead, and I should come home to answer some questions. Amber made it sound as if I was a suspect," she whispered, mostly to herself, trying to remember the conversation. "She was acting strangely, but I thought it was because David was dead. When I asked her about it though, Amber acted as if she didn't care he was murdered in their apartment."

The detective barked out his laugh, "He wasn't found in their apartment. He was found in his office; at the law firm your father owns. You are employed there?"

Reese gasped, "Up until today, yes I was employed at my father's law firm. I was fired this afternoon since I left my job with no explanation. Amber told me she found him at their apartment and called 911. Why would she lie about that?"

Detective Reyes shrugged, seeming to be as confused by the whole thing as she was. "I'm not sure why Ms. Prince would lie about where the body was discovered. Why did you leave your job with no explanation, Ms. Summers?" Reese realized the detective was still questioning her and she worried he thought she was an accomplice to David's murder.

"I've been receiving threatening letters for a few months now. May I?" Reese motioned to her handbag and the detective nodded. She pulled out the now crumpled up letter with the threatening message about Cole.

"This was the last letter I got, just before I left the city. It was sent to my office while I was at work, via private courier. I grabbed my bag and left work to pick up my son from daycare. I didn't know what else to do so I drove south, trying to come up with a good plan," she admitted.

Detective Reyes looked skeptical and she couldn't blame him. The whole thing seemed farfetched but she was living the nightmare. "Why didn't you go to the authorities or your family?" he questioned. Yeah, that was a good question but not one she was ready to answer. How did she explain she thought her father was the one behind the letter?

"I was scared and the only person I could think about going to was a man who didn't know he was a father. I headed to his condo and dumped all my problems onto the man sitting in the lobby. I told him he had a son whom he didn't know existed and do you know what he did?" Detective Reyes shook his head. "He invited us both in and took care of us. He made me feel safe and is helping me to figure out who would send me such nasty letters."

"Yes, I got from your prior speech that you two are very much in love, after what—four days together?" The detective's skepticism was back and she really couldn't blame him.

She giggled, "Yeah, I guess I started falling in love with him three years ago, but it's only been four days that we've been together. I can't explain it," she said, shrugging. "I guess when it's meant to be, it just is. I wondered if those sappy love stories were even possible. You know the ones, where the couple falls madly in love at first sight and you sit in the movie theater and roll your eyes at just how crazy it even seems. You leave the theater thinking to yourself it will never happen for you that way because love doesn't happen like that. But, I was wrong, it does—it did for me and Dane."

"Dane's the boyfriend?" the detective asked. Reese nodded her head and smiled.

"And so much more," she whispered. Detective Reyes stood, letting his metal chair scrape the floor.

"You are free to go, Ms. Summers. I'll have an officer over to your place to look into the letters you've been receiving. Hopefully, we'll be able to catch whoever is sending them to you. Don't leave the city, please." He opened the door to show her out. Reese stood and made her way across the small room.

"I can't leave the city?" she asked.

"Not until the dust settles. I may have some more questions for you," he said. "Just give the officer out front your address and I'll send someone over by morning." Reese nodded and walked to the front of the precinct to find Dane and Cole playing with a toy police car someone had given to him.

"Yook," Cole shouted, holding up the car as if it was the best thing he'd ever seen.

"Wow, you two have been having some fun out here, haven't you?" she asked her son. Cole nodded and ran back over to Dane, crawling up onto his lap.

"Everything good?" he asked, looking up at her. Reese could see the worry in his eyes and she wanted to melt into a puddle.

"Yes," she said. "They are going to send someone over to look into the letters tomorrow." Dane nodded. "I think it's time to go back to my place," she said. "No more hiding at Toni's. No more being afraid."

Dane

Dane wasn't sure if he liked Reese's idea of hiding in plain sight. They packed up their belongings and headed over to her apartment just in time to give Cole his bath and put him to bed. The toddler seemed happy to be back in his familiar surroundings even squealing when he saw his toys, rushing over to play with them. By the time they got him to sleep Dane was exhausted and he could tell Reese felt the same way.

Unfortunately, he didn't feel as comfortable in Reese's place. Her apartment was big and Dane was reminded he was out of his league. She told him she received an inheritance from her grandfather, he just wondered what that entailed. From the size of her home Reese calling herself wealthy was an understatement.

"Please make yourself at home, Dane," Reese said. She had just showered and pulled on a silky robe that made him want to run his hands all over her body.

He nodded, "Thanks," he whispered. "This is a really nice place you have here," he said, clearing his throat. Dane couldn't figure out why he was suddenly feeling nervous and shy around Reese. It probably had to do with the fact he was completely out of his element now that they were in her city and her home.

Reese seemed to be able to read his mood, wrapping her arms around his waist from behind and cuddling into his back. "It's just an apartment, Dane. No big deal," she whispered.

"I know. I guess I just didn't count on it being so—much." He looked around the room and it looked as if it belonged in one of those home magazines. "Did you decorate?" he hesitantly asked.

Reese giggled and her body rubbed against his with every breath she took. "No," she breathed. "I had someone do that for me. I'm horrible at deciding what I like and don't like. If the choice was left to me I'd have a folding table and a ratty old couch. I didn't want Cole growing up in a home that looked like a frat house. After I received my inheritance, I took a little money and made things nice for both of us." She shrugged, acting as though it wasn't a big deal.

"Well," he said clearing his throat again, "it's nice. It feels cozy, and looks nothing like a frat house," he teased.

"Mission accomplished then." Reese giggled and he pulled her to the front of his body so he could wrap her in his arms.

"The police detective called your cell while you were in the shower. I hope you don't mind that I answered it," he asked.

Reese shook her head. "No, not at all," she said. "What did he want?" Reese had already filled him in on her questioning earlier. He hated how they suspected her of having anything to do with David's death. He was also still pissed at himself for letting Amber into his condo without even so much as a second thought.

"He said an officer would be by tomorrow at around ten for information about the letters that you received. They want to open a formal case into who would want to hurt you. The detective shared that whoever sent you letters might be tied to your ex's murder." Reese gasped. Dane hated having to scare her, but he was sure she wasn't taking this whole thing as seriously as she should. They were risking a lot to be back in her apartment.

"Wow," she whispered. "I wondered if the two might be connected." Reese raised a shaky hand to her forehead. "Do you think we are safe here?" she questioned.

"I have no idea, honey. How is your security?" Dane asked. She took his hand and led him to a front office, turning on her laptop. When the screen popped up she turned it to face him.

"I had security measures installed after I received the first few letters." Dane sat down at her desk pulling Reese down onto his lap with him, needing the contact.

"This is great, honey. I'll pass this along to the guys Toni sent over." Dane could feel her whole body go rigid at the mention of Toni's security team following them to her apartment.

"Why are they here?" Reese questioned. He loved the stern look she shot him, almost as if she was scolding Cole. Honestly, it was sexy as fuck when she let her temper show but he'd never tell her that.

"As adorable as this is, baby, I already told you I won't take chances with you or Cole. I called Toni to let her know we were moving over to your place and she insisted her security detail follow us. I agreed with her and here we are." Reese tried to stand from Dane's lap and he wouldn't allow it. If she ran away from him every time he did something she didn't like they would never be in the same room with each other.

"Why didn't you tell me about this earlier?" she insisted.

"We were busy earlier. I made the call and the decision. If we are truly going to be a team here, Reese you are going to have to let me start calling some of the shots," he said. Dane wouldn't let anyone get close enough to either Reese or Cole and if he had to make the decision all over again, he would make the same one. He snooped around the station while Reese was being questioned. Cole made for a good distraction and he found an officer who was a new dad. When the young guy sat down and started talking about his newborn, Dane took his chance and asked a few questions about Reese's ex.

"There are things about David's death you don't know, Reese. If I didn't take extra precautions with you and Cole, I'd be a fool," Dane whispered.

"What things?" The worry on her beautiful face nearly did him in. He thought about not telling her about the information the tired new dad shared but he knew she would see it as a form of betrayal. They were starting a new relationship and anything but his honesty wouldn't do.

"You know he was murdered in your father's office building, not his apartment. Amber lied to us about that." Reese nodded her head, settling back into his lap and Dane had to admit he liked that she was allowing him to hold her. "He was shot in the chest but that wasn't all."

"Well, being shot to death seems like enough to me," Reese said, laughing at her own statement.

Dane chuckled and pulled her in for a quick kiss. "Sure," he agreed. "But, whoever shot him then carved the word 'cheater' into his chest."

"What? That's awful," she gasped.

"Yeah and I'm guessing that is the reason why Detective Reyes questioned you about your past relationship with David," Dane said.

"He didn't just cheat on me though," she grumbled. "David cheated on everyone he's ever been with. The man didn't have a faithful bone in his body." Dane wished Reese's ex were still alive, he'd love five minutes with him in a dark alley. He hated the asshole for the way he hurt Reese but if he hadn't, Dane would have never met her and they wouldn't have Cole.

"I've signed a statement collaborating your alibi of being at my place the night he was murdered. That will be enough to keep the detective happy, at least for a while. I'm betting Amber is somehow involved but I don't think she's working alone. They think the carving was done before David was shot. There were no signs of him being tied down. How would someone Amber's size be able to hold a grown man down and still enough to carve a word into his chest? Your ex had to have put up a fight, right?"

Reese agreed, "Yes, knowing David he would fight like hell to keep someone from doing that to him. He always prided himself on his physical appearance. Anyone trying to carve into his chest would warrant him giving them a fight. Why would anyone do that?" she cried. Dane wrapped his arms around her and pulled her down against his chest.

"I don't know, baby and I don't want to find out. Whoever did that to your ex is a monster and I'm hoping we never come face to face with the person responsible." Dane worried it would be unavoidable if the main suspect in the case turned out to be Amber. She already made contact once and he was sure that wouldn't be the last time they would hear from Reece's old friend.

Reese

The next morning, Reese wasn't roused by her overly rambunctious toddler as she usually was. She got out of bed and stumbled down the hall to his room to find he was still asleep. She quietly snuck into his room and gently pushed his hair back from his angelic face. He was always so deceptively peaceful when he slept. Reese noted he felt a little warm and sighed knowing he was probably coming down with something.

The first time Cole had gotten sick as a baby, she freaked out. Reese was alone and had no one to call for "mom advice". Her own mother had never really taken an interest in being a mom. She was far too busy being a trophy wife and running fundraisers for local charities to concern herself with how her own daughter was feeling. That job fell to the many nannies who were employed to watch and care for Reese over the years.

The first year with Cole had just about worn her down. She was feeling like a complete failure and worried she wasn't going to be able to handle being a single mother. She spent quite a few nights thinking about having a partner in raising her son, but that would mean she would have to tell Dane he was a dad.

She hired a private investigator, wanting to find out as much as possible about her son's father. Honestly, all she had to go on was his name was Dane and he was a lifeguard. Having to tell the PI she hired that she had fallen into bed with a man and all she knew was his first name and occupation was a new low for her.

It took her PI a few weeks to track Dane down and she worried he'd never turn up. A part of her hoped he had left the island and would be impossible to find. At least she could have said she tried to find him, but wouldn't have to live with the possibility of disappointment for her son or herself. When her PI called to say he found Dane Knight, her first instinct was to run down to the island and tell him he was a father. She would demand he help with Cole and take responsibility for what they had done, just as she had to do. But she was a coward.

Reese worried he would try to take Cole away from her or even reject him. The idea of Dane wanting both of them didn't seem a viable option—or at least not one she dreamed could be possible. She couldn't live with either scenario so, she did the only thing she could think of—she pulled on her supermom cape and carried on. Reese knew she wasn't the perfect mom but she was damn proud of the son she was raising. Cole was turning out to be a pretty special kid.

"Hey," Dane said, meeting her on her way out of Cole's bedroom. "Everything alright?" he whispered.

"I think he might have a little fever," she whispered. "I will take his temperature, but I'm afraid I don't have any children's fever reducer here."

"I'll run to the pharmacy, just make me a list of what you need," he said. "Is this normal? Should we call in a doctor or take him to the emergency room?" His worry was adorable, reminding Reese this was a new world for Dane. Being a father seemed to come so easily for him. Cole had taken to him with a fierceness she only saw in her son when candy or ice cream was involved. It was as if Cole sensed who Dane was and that was such a relief to her. When she showed up on Dane's doorstep, she worried the two wouldn't find the same bond she had with Cole. Seeing them together now, one would think the two had been together since Cole's birth and not just a few days.

Reese giggled, "I think he'll be fine, Dane. It's totally normal for kids to get a little fever when they are fighting off a virus. With all the traveling and being on a plane, he just picked up something," she soothed. Dane visibly exhaled.

"Thank God," he breathed. "How did you do all of this by yourself?" he asked. "I would have been a terrible single parent," he admitted.

"You would have learned to manage, just as I did. But, thank you for saying that." She went up on her tiptoes to kiss his cheek and he wrapped his arms around her waist pulling her against his body. "The first time Cole got sick, he was only six months old. I have to say, I was a nervous wreck. I actually ran him into the emergency room because my doctor's office was closed. The doctor there assured me a small fever was completely normal but I questioned every medical professional who entered our room. They must have thought I was a lunatic." She giggled at the memory. The staff was probably relieved when she was discharged to take her son home.

"They must have understood you were a scared new mother," Dane said. "I would have behaved the same way. Hell, I would have been worse." Dane grew quiet and she wondered what was going through his mind. "I've missed so much with him," he whispered. Reese could hear the sadness in his voice and it made her feel horrible. She was the reason Dane had missed so much of their son's life. It was her decision not to tell him about Cole.

"I'm so sorry, Dane," she said. "If I had to do it differently, I would have told you about Cole as soon as I found out. Can you ever forgive me?" Reese tried to pull free from his hold, but Dane wouldn't allow it. He looked down at her and smiled and he nearly took her breath away.

"Already done, baby. I wasn't ready to hear about Cole three years ago. Hell, I would have sent you packing if you had shown up on my doorstep pregnant, telling me I was going to be a daddy. I'm actually thankful you waited until now. I have a chance to make things right with both of you that I wouldn't have taken three years ago, does that make sense?" Reese nodded.

"Thank you, Dane," she whispered. He dipped his head to gently kiss her lips and her moan into his mouth had him demanding more. Dane pushed her up against the hallway wall and pressed his body against hers. Reese wrapped her legs around his waist and he ran his hands up under her t-shirt.

"Is this okay?" he asked. Reese wanted to tell him it was more than just okay, but Cole's cry felt like a bucket of cold water being thrown on them both.

Reese giggled, "Sorry," she said against his mouth. Dane smiled and put her back down on the floor.

"Let's go see what our little guy needs and then I'm going to want to revisit this whole hallway sex thing later," he teased and swatted her ass. Reese yelped and looked back at Dane.

"Deal," she promised.

K.L. Ramsey

Dane

Watching Reese with Cole these past few days always seemed to take his breath away and this morning was no exception. Their son had a fever and he didn't feel good, but Reese took control of the situation, cuddling Cole while making a list of everything they would need from the pharmacy. She really was superwoman, but telling her that would only meet with her denial. She was always so modest, but she was an awesome mother.

He quickly showered and Reese gave him directions to the closest pharmacy within walking distance. "I won't be long," he promised, taking the list she made and kissing them both. It felt so normal to be a part of them as if their little family was always in place—like it was meant to be. Dane worried he wasn't ready for the responsibility of a kid but he was wrong. Not only was he ready, it was what he had been waiting for but never had a clue he wanted.

He found the pharmacy and was in line to talk to the pharmacist about which fever reducer to get for Cole since Reese didn't specify when Amber snuck up beside him. Dane felt the hairs on his neck stand on end knowing she was possibly mixed up in David's murder.

"Hey stranger," she loudly whispered. Dane looked around the store as if trying to figure out his next move. He needed to play it cool and then he'd contact Detective Reyes to let him know about their encounter. He had a feeling there was nothing left to chance about Amber finding him.

"Hi, Amber. What are you doing back in town?" He hoped he sounded more casual than he felt. His damn heart felt as though it was going to beat out of his chest.

"I was only on the island to tell Reese about David. Once I delivered my message, I had no reason to stick around, so I came home," she insisted. "I thought I told you all that just before you so rudely threw me out of your condo." Honestly, the only thing Dane remembered from that day was the way Amber overstayed her welcome and had to be asked to leave.

"Sorry, I'm a little out of it," he said. "Cole is sick and I'm just here to pick up some medicine." Dane held up his basket as if wanting to prove his story.

"Aw, poor little guy," she offered. "Can I be of any help?" He was pretty sure she couldn't, but he didn't want to give up his hand by being rude. The more information he could get about what Amber was up to the better.

"I didn't know you're a mom, Amber." Dane was pretty sure she wasn't but he was just buying time.

Amber's scowl told him everything he needed to know. She smoothed her hands down her tailored pants suit as if accentuating her less than noticeable curves. One of Dane's new favorite things about Reese's body, after she had Cole, was her new curves.

"No," she groused. "I've not had any children. I'm concentrating on my career right now and a child would just bring my plans to a screeching halt." She looked him up and down and Dane suddenly felt a little anxious.

Luckily, it was his turn to speak with the pharmacist. "Well, it was great to see you again," Dane lied.

"Wait, Dane," she said, grabbing his arm to stop him. "How about we all get together now that you guys are in the city? I'd love to catch up with Reese since I didn't have the chance to when I visited your condo." Amber shot him an accusatory look and he shrugged.

"Sure, that would be great," he lied again.

"Before I let you go," Amber said. "How about a selfie?" Dane wanted to roll his eyes at her question. He hated selfies in general but she was taking things to a new extreme, asking him to take one with him in the middle of a pharmacy. He was a virtual stranger to her and the last time he saw her he was pretty rude. But not giving in to her request might put her off and the last thing he wanted to do was clue Amber in since he knew she was wanted by the local police department for questioning. He didn't want her to become suspicious and take off again.

"Alright," he conceded. Amber didn't miss a beat, throwing her arm around his waist and leaning into his body. She smiled and he did his best to act happy about the whole situation, although anyone who really knew him would be able to tell he was less than thrilled about taking the picture.

"Well, see you soon," she promised and turned to leave. He walked up to the pharmacy counter and tried to focus on what he needed, but he had a sinking feeling that things were about to go from zero to sixty because of his little run-in with Amber and all he wanted to do was get back to Cole and Reese.

K.L. Ramsey

Reese

Reese's phone chimed with a text and she opened the message from the unknown number. A picture of Amber and Dane popped up on her screen and she gasped. Dane looked less than thrilled to be posing for a picture with Amber and from the smug smile on her old friend's face; she was happily stirring the pot. There was no message with the picture and Reese was about to call Dane's phone when he rushed into the apartment holding his cell phone to his ear.

"I don't care if he's at lunch," Dane yelled, "This is a matter of life or death. I'm sure Detective Reyes will want to hear what I have to say." Reese felt the hairs on the back of her neck stand up and she worried Dane had a more eventful trip to the pharmacy than either of them hoped for. He shoved the bag in Reese's direction and shot her a look confirming her fears.

"Amber," she mouthed and Dane nodded. Reese took the pharmacy bag into the kitchen to get Cole his medication. They still needed to bring down his fever then they could worry about the lunatic who possibly killed her ex-fiancé. Reese woke Cole and gave him his medication, thankful Dane had remembered to get the bubblegum flavored fever reducer. Her toddler was picky and it was the only flavor he would take without argument.

"Fine, just have him call me as soon as possible. Tell him Amber Prince is back in town," Dane growled and ended the call. "How is Cole?" he questioned. Reese almost wanted to laugh, but from the look on his face, she knew better than to make light of the situation.

"He just took his medicine, thank you." Reese washed her hands and busied herself in the kitchen waiting for Dane to share about bumping into Amber at the pharmacy.

He sighed and crossed to the kitchen, pulling her into his body, "I saw her," he whispered. "Amber was at the pharmacy and I don't think it was a coincidence we happened to run into each other. I think she's watching us." Reese gasped and he hugged her closer.

"Oh my God, Dane. What if she would have hurt you?" Reese asked. The thought of Amber getting close enough to hurt Dane turned her world off its axis.

"I know, honey. I'm upset too but we just need to be careful," he soothed. "I called Toni and she is informing the head of her security about the new threat. We'll be safe here as long as we keep our heads on straight." Reese nodded against his chest, although she worried if Amber was watching them she'd also find a way to get to them, somehow. Her ex-friend was nothing if determined. It was how she ended up with David instead of Reese.

Dane's phone rang and he answered it, "Knight," he barked into the cell. "Yeah well, you really need to do something about your receptionist. I told her it was an emergency, but she refused to hunt you down." Dane sighed and looked over to where Reese had once again made herself busy tidying up the kitchen. She wished she could hear the other side of the conversation, but she also knew Dane would clue her in when he was finished. From the heavy sighing and head shaking, she was sure she wasn't going to like the recap.

Dane threw his phone up on the counter and from the look on his face, she was certain she was going to downright hate what he was about to tell her. "The detective is coming by here to question me. He wanted me to come down to the station, but I told him I wouldn't leave you knowing Amber was back in town. I also let him know Cole was running a fever and you both were my priority.

"Aww," she gushed and Dane laughed and rolled his eyes. "That's really sweet."

"Yeah well, I can be sweet," he offered. "How about you join me in the shower and I show you just how sweet I am, honey?" Reese squealed, wrapping her arms around his neck ready to take him up on his offer when Cole cried out for her.

"Sorry," she said. "When he's sick, he tends to need me more." Dane swatted her ass as she made her way down the hallway to Cole's room.

"As long as I get my turn with you later," he teased. Reese giggled and went to check on Cole. By the time she finished finding Cole's favorite stuffed dinosaur, Detective Reyes was sitting on their sofa having Dane go over his run-in with Amber. Reese joined them and listened to Dane recap the whole crazy morning.

"You were lucky that she just wanted a selfie," the detective said. "We have upgraded our search for Ms. Prince. She is our top suspect in your ex's murder." He nodded to Reese and she nodded. "Has she tried to contact you at all, Ms. Summers?" Reese nodded.

"Yes," Reese said. "Just before Dane came home Amber sent me this picture of the two of them. I didn't even know that she was back in town." Reese pulled out her phone and showed them both the picture that Amber sent to her.

"Well, if she tries to contact you again, please let me know," the detective said, standing to leave.

"What about posting a few extra guards?" Dane asked.

"I'll see what I can do but Ms. Prince hasn't threatened you, right?" Detective Reyes asked.

Dane shook his head, "Not unless you count forcing me to take a selfie with her as a threat," he grumbled. Reese giggled at the thought of anyone forcing Dane to do anything.

"I'll put in the request but I can't make you any promises," he said. Dane nodded and walked him out. Reese wondered if their lives were ever going to feel normal again. Maybe this was their new normal and she wasn't sure if she wanted to laugh or cry about that.

It had been three long days of Cole being sick. Every time his fever broke, it would spike again by dinner. Reese was exhausted but she was so thankful that she had a partner this time. Taking care of Cole with Dane had taken some getting used to but now she couldn't imagine parenting alone again. He had become her sounding board and her rock, taking care of not only Cole but of her too. She could tell that Cole's illness was starting to take its toll on Dane and she knew him well enough to know that he needed to get out of the apartment for a few hours.

"Why don't you go to my building's gym and get a workout in?" she asked. She watched as Dane considered her offer but then quickly shut her idea down.

"No," he said. "I don't want to leave you alone. I should be here in case Cole needs me." Reese smiled loving the way that he wanted to take care of them.

"I appreciate that I really do. But, you won't be any good to either of us if you don't take care of yourself," Reese said. "You'll be in the building in case we need you; I'll call and you can run back up here."

Dane seemed to think about her offer again and finally nodded. "Fine, but if either of you needs me—"

"I'll call you," she finished for him. It was almost comical how quickly Dane dressed and left for the gym. Honestly, Reese was looking forward to having a couple of hours to herself. She wanted a hot bath and some time to think about where this thing with Dane was headed. They hadn't talked about the future, but she knew that sooner or later the topic was going to come up and she wanted to be ready. Cole was napping on the sofa and she wanted to take advantage of her free time. She had so many questions to consider; from where they would live to if she could live with Dane's dangerous job as a firefighter. She knew he was good at his job, but the couple times that he was called out to a fire while she was living on the island made her anxiety spike. Reese felt silly for worrying about a man she barely knew, but she had and she was betting that wouldn't change, especially now that they were together.

Reese heard a rustling at the front door and smiled, knowing that Dane had probably forgotten his key again. "Did you forget your key again, babe?" she asked, pulling open the door. Amber smiled at her and Reese scurried to shut the door.

"Now Reese, is that any way to treat your best friend?" Reese instinctively backed up at the sight of Amber's gun, pointing straight at her chest.

"We aren't friends," Reese spat. "We haven't been friends since you decided to sleep with my fiancé on my wedding day." Amber chuckled and shook her head.

"Always such a bitch," Amber chided. "I won't wait for you to invite me in. Your manners are a little rusty." Amber strode into Reese's apartment as if she owned the place, backing Reese up as she entered with the gun.

"What do you want, Amber?" Reese asked. Amber looked around her apartment as if taking in her surroundings.

"Who is here with us, Reese? I'm assuming your brat is nearby, but where is that hunky firefighter of yours?" Amber asked.

"Cole is sleeping on the sofa; he's been sick. Dane isn't here," Reese said.

"Perfect," Amber purred. "That gives us girls some time to talk and come up with a good plan. You're going to need to do exactly what I tell you to do or I'll have to kill that adorable brat of yours." Reese sobbed, not caring that she was giving away her hand. The thought of Amber hurting her son was terrifying to her.

"I'll do whatever you want, Amber. There will be no need to hurt my son. Please, just tell me what you want me to do and leave Cole out of it." Reese knew she was begging but she didn't give a fuck. She would beg and plead with Amber to leave Cole and Dane alone if she had to.

Amber chuckled as if she was enjoying watching Reese squirm and beg. "Oh Reese, how I've missed our friendship," she said. "I'm going to need for you to get rid of your boyfriend when he gets back. If you tell him that I'm here or try to clue him in, in any way, I will kill him and Cole."

"I understand," Reese whispered. "If I can convince Dane to take Cole with him, will you let them both go?" she asked. Amber acted as if she was thinking over Reese's request.

"Sure," she agreed. "I'll be a good sport and let your brat go with his father. I really hate children and not having to drag the screaming little bastard along with us will be so much easier." Cole stirred on the sofa and fell back to sleep. Amber motioned for Reese to move down the hallway. "Let's go back to your room and finish our conversation," she ordered. "I really don't want to wake the brat." Reese was fine with that idea. The further away Amber was from Cole the better.

"We can wait for your hunky firefighter to get back and then you will have one chance to get rid of them both," Amber said, shoving Reese down to sit on the bed. "Otherwise, I'll get rid of them my way," she promised.

K.L. Ramsey

Dane

Dane walked into Reese's apartment thinking about how much it was beginning to feel like home. He wouldn't mind living in New York and knew that there was always a need for fireman in the city, but they hadn't discussed anything permanent yet. The past few days had felt like a whirlwind with Cole being sick and Reese trying to take care of him. He had to run down to the police station again earlier that morning to answer yet another round of Detective Reyes's questions. He hated that they were still in the middle of the shit storm but since his run in with Amber, he had been called in and questioned more than a few times. Luckily, Reese could remain at home with Cole since his fever was still hanging on and Dane had always made sure they were heavily guarded. Just that morning, Cole's fever seemed to finally break for good and Dane had to admit it felt as though he could breathe again. Cole being sick made him feel completely helpless but Reese handled it like a champ, even insisting he use her building's gym to blow off some steam. Dane felt better after working off some of the extra stress that had built up since they got into

New York and now he was ready to conquer the world—after a quick shower.

Reese walked out from their bedroom to find him in the hallway. She jumped as if he startled her. "Dane, what are you doing back?" she asked.

"I've been gone for almost two hours, baby," he said, pulling her into his sweaty body. "It hurts my feelings that you didn't miss me," he teased. Reese swatted at him and made a noise letting him know that she wasn't into sweaty guys fresh from the gym. Dane released her, noting the flash of panic in her eyes when he went to open the door to their room.

"Wait," she shouted. "What are you going to do?" Reese pulled his hand away from the door knob and every one of his instincts was telling him something was wrong. It was as if Reese was trying to keep him out of their bedroom. She shook her head at him as if trying to signal for him not to ask her any questions and he decided to play along.

"Why don't you come into the family room? Cole is watching cartoons and we have a few things to discuss," she said. Dane could tell from her expression he wasn't going to like the discussion they were about to have.

"Alright honey. Whatever you want," he agreed.

"I have something that I need to say to you," she all but shouted at him. "I saw the pictures of you and Amber. She sent them to me and I know everything," Reese shouted. Dane was starting to realize that his instincts were correct and whatever was going on, he wasn't going to like it.

Reese led the way into the kitchen and grabbed a piece of paper and a pen, not skipping a beat in their conversation. "I'm not sure what Amber sent over, honey. I told you that I saw her at the pharmacy a few days ago and she asked me to take a selfie with her."

Reese scribbled something onto the paper and shoved it in his direction. "Yeah, well the picture that she sent over was a hell of a lot hotter than just a selfie," Reese cried.

Amber is in the bedroom and has a gun. Just play along and get Cole out of here. She just wants me.

Dane read the note and felt a wave of panic. There was no fucking way that he would be able to walk out of that apartment without Reese but the pleading look in her eyes nearly did him in. She looked over to where Cole was quietly watching cartoons on the sofa and back to him as if silently asking him to choose their son. There had to be a better plan.

Reese pulled the paper back in front of her to continue their conversation so Amber wouldn't catch on to her silently letting him know about the danger they were all in. "I want for you to leave, Dane. I need you to take Cole and just go. I need time to think about what I want." She was so convincing his heart ached.

"What the fuck, honey?" he questioned. If they were going to get Amber to believe that he'd so easily walk away from the love of his life, they were going to need to do a better job of selling their argument.

Reese shoved the note at him again and he quickly scanned it.

Please, I need to know Cole is safe. Call for help once you get him out. I'll be fine.

Dane knew that her last statement was a guess at best and a part of him wanted to refuse but she was right, he had to get Cole out of there. He could call for help and if that took too long he'd go in after Reese himself because there was no fucking way that he was going to let Amber hurt her. Reese was his life but he'd do this her way.

Cole stood and crossed to where they were both talking in the kitchen, smiling up at Dane and taking his hand as if he knew his part in Reese's crazy plan. Amber getting her hands on Cole was out of the question and he nodded basically agreeing to walk away from her; leaving Reese in the hands of someone who probably was a killer and would take great pleasure in hurting her. The thought of that happening almost made him change his mind, but Cole's small hand in his own reminded him that his son had to come first.

Reese mouthed the words "thank you" to Dane and he nodded, dipping his head to quietly kiss her lips. Reese knelt to kiss Cole's little head hiding her sob so that Amber wouldn't catch on. They had a show to put on if they were going to convince Amber that he was really leaving. It was now or never.

Reese

"You can't believe I am interested in Amber, Reese. It's fucking ridiculous. She's lying and you should trust me enough to know that by now. Have these past two weeks meant nothing to you? We're a family now or at least I thought we were." It gutted Reese to hear the anger and betrayal in his voice but she knew that it was all just for show. There was no other way to get Dane and Cole out of her apartment but to convince Amber that they were breaking up. Amber was hiding in her bedroom waiting for her to fuck up and she wasn't going to give her the chance to hurt either of her guys. She pushed Cole's hair back from his eyes and kissed his forehead. Her son could tell something was wrong, but he was happily playing with his toy cars while watching her and Dane.

"Please Dane, just take Cole and go. I need time to think about everything." Reese hoped she sounded convincing but honestly she wasn't sure. "I don't know what to believe anymore and I just need a few hours to think things through. Take him and go out or go back to Toni's place, please," she begged. The way Dane was watching her, she wasn't sure if he'd follow through with her plan or if he'd change his mind. If they didn't sell this performance they were all in danger. She believed Amber when she threatened to kill Dane and Cole. Reese was sure that Amber had murdered David in cold blood, so she knew Amber was capable of anything.

"What's going on here, Reese? Please just talk to me; tell me what Amber said." Reese wasn't sure what to tell Dane to make it all sound believable. She just knew it was going to have to be one crazy whopper of a lie to make it seem that Dane would take Cole and walk away from her.

"Amber called me earlier and told me that the other morning when you ran to the store to get Cole his medication, you two hooked up. She sent me pictures and everything, Dane. How could you do that to me? I thought you said you were done with meaningless hook-ups, but I guess that just proves I was a fool for believing you. I should have known you haven't changed. You're the same man I met three years ago. All you want is a good time in the sack and then you leave. I won't be that for you, Dane. I told you I don't do sloppy seconds." She glanced up at Dane and saw the hurt and pain in his eyes and regretted her words. Reese sent him a pleading look trying to let him know that she didn't mean any of it. She was sure she had said enough to make their argument sound convincing for Amber, but worried about what it just cost her. The sadness in his eyes nearly tore her in two and all she wanted to do was wrap her arms around him and tell him she was sorry. Doing so would be a big mistake and cost her the two people she loved most in the world. They needed to keep up the façade that he was leaving her or Amber would make good on her threats.

"So what now, Reese? I give you time to think, but it seems you have already made up your mind about me—about us." Dane was breathing hard as if he had just run a race and Reese could tell he was holding back. She wanted to tell him that she was sorry for saying such hateful words to him and that she'd be alright as long as he and Cole were safe, but she couldn't.

Reese knew this might be the last time she would see either of them and all she wanted to do was tell them both how much she loved them. She picked up Cole and hugged him to her body. "I just need a few hours to really wrap my head around all of this, Dane. Can you please take Cole with you and at least give me that?" She kissed his soft cheek and didn't hide the sob that escaped her.

"Fine Reese, I'll take Cole and we'll go to Toni's for a few hours but I'm coming back. I won't let you push me away and I won't let you believe a lunatic over me. You take your few hours to think about what Amber told you. But when I get back, you and I are going to sit down and you're going to listen to my side of the story. I love you, Reese," he whispered. She closed her eyes trying to hide the tears that were threatening to spill down her cheeks. She wanted to say those words back to him but she couldn't. All Reese could muster was a head nod and he took Cole from her arms. She watched as Dane helped him on with his jacket and gathered his bag and she wondered if those were the last words she would ever speak to him. Dane turned to look back at her as if waiting for her to change her mind or tell him she loved him too but she didn't—she couldn't.

Dane turned to leave with Cole in his arms and the door shut behind them. Reese watched her world walk out her apartment door and all she could do was let them go. "I love you too," she whispered.

"Aww, how sweet." Amber's sing-song voice made Reese want to vomit. She turned to find her old friend with the gun trained on her again. Panic welled up inside of her and she knew there would be no one coming to her rescue, no one running in to save her. Reese was going to have to save herself if she ever wanted to see Dane or Cole again.

"I did as you asked, Amber. Now, tell me what you want so we can get this over with," she ordered. Reese knew she was pushing her luck giving Amber orders, but she didn't want to spend any more time with the crazy woman than was necessary.

Amber made a tsking sound as if she didn't approve of Reese's tone. "Is that any way to talk to the person who holds your whole future in the palm of her hands?" Amber asked, waving the gun around. "You and I are going on a little trip,

Reese. If you behave yourself, I'll let you go and you can run back to your fireman and bastard son. If not, I'll make sure you end up just like David."

"You killed him didn't you?" Reese asked, even though she was sure she already knew the answer.

Amber's laugh mocked her. "Of course I did, you stupid bitch. He cheated on me and I won't be with a man who cheats."

"You do know he cheated on me to be with you, right?" Reese questioned. It was Reese's turn to laugh and she was sure Amber wasn't finding the whole thing quite as funny anymore. "How's that old saying go? Once a cheater, always a cheater. You knew what you were getting with David, Amber and yet you still eagerly jumped into his bed. I wonder why that was. I'm guessing you've always secretly hated me or wanted to be me." Reese shrugged, "Either way makes you a pathetic loser." Amber gasped and took a step back as if Reese physically attacked her.

"How dare you, Reese? I was your friend but you wouldn't know what a friend looks like, would you? You always were an ungrateful bitch. You didn't deserve David." Amber was starting to show her hand, coming undone at the seams a little. Reese hoped if she could keep her talking she'd be able to distract her enough to figure out a way to escape.

"So, you just took him off my hands then? Did you really see stealing my fiancé as an act of goodwill on your part, Amber?" Reese watched as Amber's nerve seemed to steady and she worried she had miscalculated her old friend.

"You think this is all about you, don't you Reese? Of course, you do," Amber shrieked. "You think everything is about you." Amber's laugh was mean. "You are just a pawn in a bigger game, Reese. We just need for you to access a few accounts for us and then you can walk away and keep your fucking mouth shut or meet the same fate as poor David. He figured out what we were doing and it didn't bode well for him."

Reese was trying to follow along but Amber wasn't making much sense. "We?" Reese questioned. "Who are you working with, Amber?" She remembered Dane's theory. If Amber was the killer she would have to be working with someone. Dane said the autopsy said the word "cheater" was carved into David's chest before he was shot. If that was the case, Amber wouldn't have had the strength to hold David down to cut him. He would have most likely put up a fight and she would have needed someone else there to hold David down. Probably a man and knowing Amber, someone who she was sleeping with. Amber ran through men like they were wearing expiration dates. Reese was surprised to hear she and David had lasted as long as they had.

Amber flashed Reese her wicked smile. "Don't you worry that pretty little head of yours, Reese. I'm sure my partner will make an appearance at some point. For now, you and I are going to take a little ride together." Reese knew it was a bad idea to go anywhere with Amber, but she also knew that Dane was hopefully calling in backup and would find her.

"Let's go," Amber nodded to the door and Reese turned to leave. She wished she could leave some sign for Dane but it would be impossible. The best she could hope for now was somewhere along the line Amber would fuck up and she'd get her chance to escape. Reese was going to have to save herself, no more playing the damsel in distress.

K.L. Ramsey

Dane

Dane pulled his pick-up around the block and parked it making sure he had a good vantage point to see all the cars going in and out of Reese's apartment building's garage. He checked his rearview mirror to see Cole happily playing with his cars and smiled. His son had no idea what was happening and he hoped to keep it that way. If his hunch was correct, Amber would be moving Reese quickly and he wanted to be ready to follow. He hated hearing her tell him the words that he feared she would say to him someday. He wasn't that same man she met three years ago and he also knew Reese was finding a way to make their argument believable but her words stung. Dane knew that he was being foolish but it was how he felt.

Walking away from Reese, leaving her with a crazy woman that probably wanted to hurt her or worse, was the hardest thing he'd ever had to do. He just needed to work out a plan and call for some help. Otherwise, Amber would win and that was unacceptable to him. He loved Reese for wanting to keep him and Cole safe, he really did but she was now in horrible danger.

Dane decided he was finished taking chances and not trusting his gut. It was time to call in the cavalry. He dialed Detective Reyes's number and hoped like hell he picked up. Every second that ticked by was one more that he left the woman that he loved in the hands of a mad woman.

"Reyes," he barked into the phone.

"Yes, this is Dane Knight," Dane responded.

"The boyfriend," Detective Reyes said, not giving him time to protest that he was more than just Reese's fucking boyfriend. "I take it you have heard from Ms. Prince again," he asked.

"Yes and no," Dane offered. "She has Reese now at our apartment. She somehow got to Reese while I was at the gym. Reese staged a fight between the two of us to give me an excuse to walk away with Cole, but they are still in there." He knew he must have sounded crazy but Dane didn't give a shit. "Amber has a gun. Please, detective, I can't lose her."

"Give me the details and I'll get some men on this," he said. "We'll get to Ms. Summers, I promise."

"Thank you," Dane said. He just hoped they weren't all too late because he couldn't lose Reese again. Not now, not after he just found her after three long years. Dane filled the detective in on everything that had just happened and he agreed to send over a team of officers, but the detective worried the same thing as Dane that Amber was going to move her. The last thing Dane wanted to do was wait around for help to show up, but he was useless having Cole tagging along.

He ended the call with Detective Reyes and dialed Toni. She picked up on the first ring. "Tell me everything is good," Toni said into the other line. Dane smiled at the way his friend worried about him. He knew he could always count on her.

"I need a favor," Dane said. "I need someone to watch Cole and I'm not sure who to trust. Any suggestions?"

Toni sighed into her end of the phone. "I'm guessing you're not going to fill me in?" she asked.

"No time. Reese is in danger and I can't go after her with Cole in tow. I need someone safe, someone, you trust," he said.

"I'll have my head of security, Troy Davis, meet you at Reese's apartment," she offered. "He's a dad and one of the people I trust most in New York. I know he'll guard Cole with his life."

"Thanks for that," Dane whispered. "I'll meet him at the parking garage across the street from Reese's apartment. It's a long story and I don't have time to go into it right now, but she is being held by the crazy woman who killed Reese's ex."

"Oh God," Toni cried. "Please be careful, Dane. I'll have Troy meet you as soon as possible. And if anything happens to any of you Dane, I'll personally come up there and kick your ass," Toni scoffed, causing him to chuckle. He ended the call knowing she meant every word and he was grateful for his friend.

K.L. Ramsey

Reese

Amber nudged Reese towards a waiting black SUV and shoved her into the driver's seat. "You'll drive so I can keep an eye on you, Reese. Don't go getting any ideas or playing the hero," Amber said. "We take this all nice and easy and you get to go back to your quiet, mundane existence and I'll be off on some island sipping one of those fancy little drinks with an umbrella in it."

"So, its money you want then?" Reese asked. "I'm good with that; I have plenty to give you. We can just head down to my bank and I can—" Amber didn't let her finish her thought, slamming the car door in her face and quickly rounding the car to get into the passenger seat.

"Sorry Reese, was that rude?" Amber asked with a smirk on her face. "I just got bored with you thinking you call the shots. I'm the one in charge here."

Reese smiled, "Sure, Amber. You're in charge." Reese nodded. "Keys?" she asked. Amber handed them over and Reese started the car taking her time to adjust the seat and mirrors. She was trying to buy all the time possible hoping Dane would find a way to get to her.

"Stop stalling," Amber ordered. "Let's just get a move on. I need you to head down to your father's office building."

Reese did a double take. "Why are we going there?" She asked.

"Because that is where the papers are that you will be signing. We just need your signature and then you'll be free to go," Amber promised. Reese was starting to believe she was never going to be free of Amber or her plan.

"Does my father know about all of this?" Reese questioned. Amber remained silent beside her and she was sure she had guessed correctly. Her father was somehow involved in this mess.

"Was it you or him who sent me the letters?" Reese asked, trying to piece it all together.

"Well, it was a collaborative effort," Amber proudly admitted. "At first, it was your dad. He came up with the idea of scaring you and then when we got you good and upset he was going to demand you meet and sign the papers. But, as time went on you seemed to grow bolder. It was almost as if you defied us so that we would come after you. When Robert started to chicken out about taking what we needed from you by any means necessary, I stepped in," Amber admitted.

"Why, why would either of you do that to me?" Reese asked. Amber laughed.

"You really have no clue, do you?" Reese knew the way to the office by heart. If they kept going at the rate they were she was going to run out of time. Once she got to the office she was sure her luck would run out and she'd face the same fate as David. She wanted to laugh at the irony of actually feeling sorry for David, but she did.

"I have no clue as to why two people I was closest to would want to hurt me or my son," Reese admitted. She was hoping for one of New York's famous traffic jams but she was out of luck. She was even making every green light.

"I think I'll let Robert have the pleasure of telling you what's been going on right under your nose. He'll appreciate the chance to bring you to your knees. You've always been a thorn in your father's side, Reese," Amber spat. Reese knew the girl who she grew up with, her best friend since grade school—that girl was gone. Beside her sat a cold-hearted bitch that slept with her best friend's fiancé and showed no remorse over it. She was a killer, someone capable of snuffing out another's life and Reese needed to remember she was probably next on Amber's list.

They drove the rest of the way to her father's office in silence. Reese had so many questions but honestly, she wanted to ask them of her dad. She wanted to look the man who raised her in the eyes and ask him why he hated her so much.

"Park in your father's space. He's left explicit instructions on what we are to do," Amber said.

"How did this little partnership between you two happen?" Reese asked. She slowly pulled into her father's reserved space and put the car in park in no hurry to go into the building.

"After I grew tired of David, your father and I hooked up a few times," Amber admitted.

Reese suddenly felt sick. Was everyone sleeping with her ex-fiancé and her father? No wonder her dad seemed fine with the fact that David was fucking all of her friends. Her father was doing the same thing.

"How romantic," she drawled.

Amber seemed to swoon and Reese rolled her eyes at her theatrics. "It was actually very romantic," Amber gushed. "Robert really knows how to sweep a woman off of her feet."

"Sure and make her do his dirty work. You know my father is a very cunning man. He's using you to get to me. He wants something from me and he's using you to do all his heavy lifting. I'm assuming he's been calling the shots, telling you where to go and what to do? Was it really his idea to send you to find me?" Reese needed to keep Amber talking to buy time. If she was correct the black pick-up truck sitting across the street from her apartment building was Dane's rental. Hopefully, he was able to call in the cavalry in time. She just needed to buy them some time to get into place.

"Yes," Amber spat. "It was Robert's brilliant plan to send me down to that island. And, it worked too—here you are. He was hoping you'd leave the brat and your baby daddy out of this though. Having them both tag along has really slowed down our plans." Amber pulled down the sun visor to check her reflection in the mirror, her gun trained on Reese the entire time. Reese wanted to make a play for it but at this close proximity, if the gun went off it would definitely hit her and she couldn't take the chance.

"Ugh, I'm a wreck," Amber whispered.

"Yeah, kidnapping someone at gunpoint really takes its toll on you," Reese sassed, seeming to ramp up Amber's bad mood.

"Let's go," Amber insisted. "Nice and slow. I wouldn't want to put any holes in your designer jacket," she warned. Reese undid her seatbelt and slowly got out of the car, holding her hands above her head.

"Put your hands down," Amber hissed. "This isn't an episode of Cops and you'll draw undue attention to us."

"Well, we wouldn't want that now, would we?" Reese dryly asked.

They made their way into the building and directly passed security where the guard waved them through. To anyone looking on they were just two old friends hanging out together. Amber had pulled Reese close and slung her arm around her shoulder, shoving the barrel of the gun into her side. They got into her father's private elevator and Amber released her as if she couldn't stand being so close to her either.

When the elevator doors opened her father was standing on the other side with a gun in his hand, pointed right at her. "Geeze, I'm starting to feel a little left out," she grumbled. "Everyone seems to have a gun except me. Is it a new fashion accessory that I'm not aware of, Daddy?" Reese spat his name with all the pent-up contention she felt for her father.

"You always have a smart assed response for every situation, don't you Reese?" he asked. "I'm sure that by the time we are finished here you'll find yourself less witty." Amber stepped behind her, shoving the barrel of the gun into her back effectively pushing her towards her father.

"Why am I here?" Reese demanded. Her father's laugh was mean and she was starting to get the feeling that whatever he had planned for her, telling her his intentions wasn't a part of it.

"You'll find out soon enough," her father taunted her. "Shall we?" He led the way into his office and pointed at the chair where he wanted for Reese to sit.

"I'd like to just get whatever you have planned for me over with. I have plans and I'd like to get back to them," Her father laughed again and she wished he would stop toying with her.

Pushing wasn't the best option either but she was beginning to tire of his secrecy.

"I had a feeling you might want to push things along so I had the papers ready for you to sign." Robert pushed the stack of papers towards her and handed her a pen. "Sign," he ordered.

"Well Daddy, what kind of lawyer would I be if I didn't at least read the documents I was about to sign?" she taunted. Reese picked up the papers from his desk and started to read them over.

"We really don't have time for this, Robert. I'm pretty sure her boyfriend didn't buy the whole speech she gave him about needing him to give her time," Amber loudly whispered. Reese smiled knowing her old friend was right. Dane would never believe she'd just push him out of her life; not without good reason.

"I think he might show up here looking for her. We need those papers signed and to be long gone before that happens," Amber warned. Her father's frustrated growl rang through the office causing her to giggle. She loved that his plan was starting to unravel and she had front row seats to watch. From what she was gathering about the papers they wanted her to sign, he was out of money as well as time.

"I see you want me to sign over my inheritance from my grandfather. Tell me, Daddy how long have you been broke?"

She was guessing, but judging from the sour expression on her father's face Reese hit the nail on the head with her assumption.

"You have no idea what it takes to run a corporation, Reese. You never had the business savvy to know the ins and outs of my world and you never will. You're just a grunt collecting paychecks and you'll never amount to anything more. I had such high hopes for you when you were a child but then you turned out to be just as disappointing as your mother. I wanted a son from her but all she ever gave me was you—just one major disappointment after another." Reese knew his words should hurt her but they didn't. In fact, she found his little speech quite funny.

"No, Daddy don't hold back." She laughed. "Please, tell me how you really feel," she sassed.

Her father's smile was mean as he sat on the corner of his desk keeping his gun trained on her. He seemed to think he was more intimidating at eye level but he was wrong. "When I convinced David to marry you, offering him everything he could ever dream of having or becoming, I thought my troubles with you were over. I was handing you both a better life on a silver platter but you both seemed to fuck it up. I knew if I held David's strings, I'd be able to control the inheritance you were about to receive. When you walked away from him all hope was lost, or so I thought. You ended up pregnant and I knew that sooner or later you would let your guard down and I'd be able to get to you through your son. I just hadn't planned on you running back to the man who you made your biggest mistake with, to help do your bidding.

"Yeah, Dane has a way of throwing a monkey wrench into everyone's plans. I certainly didn't plan on falling into bed with him three years ago or having his baby—but here we are." She loved the bitter expression on her father's face every time she mentioned Dane or the way she let him take her. It made him so angry that she allowed someone like Dane to touch her, let alone exist in her world. Reese wondered how her father would feel knowing she had fallen in love with Dane. But, that was too personal to share with someone who was holding a gun at her chest.

"You have certainly hit rock bottom, My Dear. And now, you will pay for every bad decision you have ever made," he warned.

"What happens if I don't sign the papers, Daddy? Have you thought about that?" she asked. His evil smile told her he had planned for something like that and she wasn't going to like what he had come up with.

"I've given that a great deal of thought, Reese. If you don't sign those papers I will kill you and then go after Cole. Any court would give him to me over his low-life father and I would have direct access to your fortune through him. Maybe he'll grow up to be less of a disappointment than you have—but I doubt it." Reese gasped, knowing he wasn't leaving her much choice. Either way, she couldn't imagine he'd leave her alive. At least if she signed the papers Cole would have a chance to grow up happy with Dane.

"Fine," she said. She snatched the pen from the desk and worked her way through the papers initialing and signing where indicated. Her father seemed to grow more impatient with every second that ticked on.

Reese finished signing the papers and threw them, along with the pen, back onto the desk. "Now what, Daddy? We both know you won't just let me walk out of here. I'm assuming my fate will be much like David's." Reese wasn't really asking as much as guessing.

"That is up to you," he said. "I'm pretty sure you won't be able to keep your big mouth shut so I'd like to err on the side of caution." Amber helped her up and she stood between the two of them sure that she was about to draw her last breath.

"Take her down by the river this time, Amber and don't play with her like you did David. I'd like for this all to be finished today." Her father's cold tone shouldn't have surprised her but it had. How could a parent hate his own flesh and blood so much? She would have done anything in her power to keep her little boy safe while her own father was basically ordering her execution.

"What about us, Robert? Where are we meeting?" Amber's tone sounded as though she was worried.

"I'll be in touch, Amber," he said, effectively dismissing her. "Now, do as I've instructed." Reese heard Amber's sob and knew her father's promise sounded just as empty to her.

"You promised we can be together now. You told me you'd leave your wife and you and I would start over. Has that changed?" Amber questioned. She stepped from behind Reese and faced Robert head on seeming to need answers from Reese's father.

"Oh Amber," Robert chided her and Reese wanted to tell her old friend to run, to get out of there because she knew that tone. He was at the end of his rope and she was going to be effectively dismissed. Reese just worried how her father would dismiss Amber. He pointed his gun at her and before Amber could protest, he shot her in the chest.

Reese lunged forward as if she was going to catch her former friend from hitting the floor, instead, she grabbed her gun. She yanked it from Amber's hand as she fell to the ground and turned to point it at her father.

"Put the gun down, Reese," he commanded. "I will not hesitate to shoot you too," her father threatened. Sadly, she believed every word. He would easily end her life and he would show no remorse after he was done.

Reese heard a commotion out in the hall and was sure from the sound of it that a whole army was about to invade. Instead, Dane came rushing into her father's office. Everything seemed to move at warp speed and before she knew what was happening, her father pointed his gun at Dane and fired. The bullet sliced through Dane's side and he stumbled backward. Before her dad could get another shot off, she turned and shot him in the chest. He looked at her in disbelief and honestly, she felt the same way. Reese had shot her own father, but there was no way she'd let him take another shot at Dane. She dropped the gun and rushed to Dane's side, covering his blood stained shirt with her hand.

"I'm so sorry, Dane," she whispered. He tried to smile at her but winced in pain.

"You didn't shoot me, honey," Dane choked. She could tell he was in pain, but she had no idea what to do. "Put pressure on it. Help is on the way," he whispered.

"Isn't that supposed to be my line?" she teased.

Dane laughed and grabbed his side. "Ouch. Don't make me laugh, honey," he grumbled. "Sorry it took me so long but I had to arrange daycare."

"Cole?" she asked, looking around as if he'd be there. She knew better than to believe Dane would put their son in danger and drag him to her father's office.

"He's safe. Toni had her head of security babysit." Reese nodded. A team of police officers swarmed into the office and Reese breathed a sigh of relief.

"He's hurt," she shouted. "My father shot him." An EMT filed into the room and took Reese's place, essentially pushing her out of the way.

"The bullet might have hit a kidney," the EMT said. "We'll have him to the hospital in no time," he promised. Reese nodded.

"There are two bodies over here," an officer yelled. Reese knew she was going to have to go downtown to answer questions, but all she wanted to do was go with Dane to the hospital. Detective Reyes walked into the office and nodded in her direction as soon as he saw her.

"Ms. Summers," he said. "I think you know what I'm going to say next." The detective looked over to where the EMTs were working on Dane and she sobbed.

"Please just let me go to the hospital with him. As soon as I know he's alright I'll come downtown to answer all of your questions," she pleaded.

He looked at Amber's body and then back to her. "Mr. Knight said that she abducted you?" he asked.

Reese nodded. "At gunpoint," she added. "My father and Amber were working together this whole time. He was broke and he was trying to get my inheritance my grandfather left me.

He forced me to sign those papers," she said, nodding to the desk where the contracts sat. "But he was hasty and didn't check my signature." Detective Reyes crossed the office and picked up the paperwork reading over the last page. He laughed and pointed to her and Reese wasn't sure if she was in trouble or if she had done something right.

"Well, he would have been very displeased once he noticed you signed the paperwork, "Reese's Pieces," he said, chuckling to himself.

"Yeah, it used to be my nickname. I knew it wouldn't stand up in a court of law and he wouldn't look twice at the signature since it looked like my first name." She shrugged. Dane groaned as they loaded him onto the gurney and she made her way through the sea of people to be by his side.

"I'll have a police officer escort you to the hospital, Ms. Summers. You can be questioned there," Detective Reyes offered.

"Thank you," she said. "For everything." Reese took Dane's hand and squeezed it in her own.

"I'll be right behind you, Dane," she promised.

K.L. Ramsey

Dane

Dane woke up, squinting against the bright florescent lights of the room. He tried to remember where he was or what happened to him as he groggily searched his surroundings. He looked down at his body and realized he must be in the hospital, judging from all the tubes and machines beeping and making noise.

As if on cue, his memories of rushing into Robert Summer's office, to find Reese pointing a gun at her father and vice versa, came rushing back. He hated the fear he saw on her beautiful face when she crouched by his side trying to stop the bleeding from the gunshot wound her father caused. His only regret was he hadn't shot Robert himself. Reese must be feeling so much guilt at having had to kill her own father; he wished he could have done that for her so she wouldn't have to live with it.

He looked around the room and found Reese sleeping in a very uncomfortable looking chair in the corner. She had a light blanket thrown over her body and her head propped up on a pillow. Cole was asleep on the sofa next to her and from the looks of it his son was pretty comfortable all sprawled out, unlike his mama. He chuckled and groaned at the pain that shot through his side, waking Reese.

"You're awake," she whispered, sitting up straighter in the chair. She stood and stretched, crossing to his bed. "I'll call the nurse," she offered, pushing a button on his bed.

"How long have I been out?" he asked. His voice sounded like he had swallowed glass and Reese helped him take a sip of water.

"Almost two days," she whispered. "I was so worried." Dane reached for her hand and she gently took his.

"Sorry I worried you, baby. What's the damage?" he asked. He could tell they had to do some work to his side because it hurt like a son of a bitch.

"You were lucky, the bullet missed your kidney but you lost your spleen. The doctor said that you can live without that though." Reese's voice was so quiet, he worried that she had suffered much more than him.

"How are you doing with everything that happened?" he asked. Reese shrugged as if shooting her father wasn't a big deal. The story behind her eyes told him otherwise. She was sad and hurting and he wished like hell that there was something he could do about it.

"I'm fine," Reese said.

"Liar," he teased. "Talk to me, tell me how you're really feeling, Reese."

She exhaled again but this time she didn't try to put up her walls. "I'm sick of everyone asking me how I am. I wish I could put this whole crazy saga behind me but I'm constantly reminded that my father killed my ex-fiancé, my ex-best friend and tried to kill me. Add in the fact he shot the man that I love and it's enough to drive me over the edge. But, I can't lose it. I have a son to take care of and a life to piece back together."

Dane didn't want to push her, but he wondered if the life that she was piecing back together involved him. Now that everything was over and she and Cole were safe again, he worried his function in their lives had changed. What if she didn't need him anymore since she was safe? He wondered where all of these changes left him.

"You'll be in here for about another week," Reese whispered. "Where is that nurse?" she nervously asked, looking over her shoulder.

"Reese," he whispered. "I'm fine." He felt anything but fine. Dane felt unsure of himself and their relationship and he wished he could get out of the fucking hospital bed and pull her into his arms to remind her just what she meant to him. They had come too far to take so many steps backward but that was exactly what was happening.

Reese impatiently pressed the button again to call the nurse and she came rushing into the room. "I'm coming," she grumbled. "Well, look whose awake—welcome back Mr.

Knight," she said, smiling down at him. "How's the pain?" she asked.

"Bearable," he lied. Actually, it felt like someone was stabbing him in the side, but admitting that would get him a hefty dose of pain meds and he had some things he wanted to say to Reese.

"I'm not going to flat out call you a liar," the nurse chided. "But I'm pretty sure that you could use a dose of pain medicine."

"Just take your medication, Dane," Reese said. "We will have plenty of time to talk when you wake up. Besides, I need to take Cole home and feed him some dinner. We will be back tomorrow when you are feeling up to a visit. He's been anxious to see you," she whispered. Reese lightly kissed his lips and turned to gather her things. Dane wanted to tell her not to go but he could see her putting her walls firmly back into place. He hated how she was shutting him out again but there was nothing he could do about it. The drugs that his nurse shot into his IV were starting to take effect and his head felt foggy. He watched as Reese gently woke Cole and the two of them left his room. Dane wanted to call them back but instead, he let the darkness consume him once again as he drifted off to sleep.

K.L. Ramsey

Reese

It had been just over a week since Dane was shot and having him back home at her apartment felt like a self-imposed prison. She wasn't sure what to do about all of the new feelings that were plaguing her, telling her she didn't deserve happiness. She heard her father's voice telling her over and over saying she was unworthy. Having Dane around made her feel as if the floor was going to fall out of her world at any moment and there would be nothing she could do about it.

Dane was starting to feel like his old self again and getting antsier by the day. She knew that sooner or later he was going to want to return home and Reese worried about where that would leave the two of them. She knew long distance relationships didn't work. Sure, they would make each other promises but in the end, they would break things off and Cole would be the one to suffer. She knew breaking things off with Dane now would hurt like hell but in the long run, it would be easier for her son.

"Hey, what would you like to do for dinner tonight?" Dane asked. Reese sat down on the sofa next to him knowing that if she didn't say what she needed to, she never would.

"I think we have other things to talk about besides dinner," she whispered. Dane leaned in closer as if trying to hear her and she stood needing some distance. She was going to just say it—get it out in the open. Otherwise, she never would and then where would she be? Almost losing Dane taught her one thing—that eventually, she would. Sure her father wasn't a threat anymore but his job was a dangerous one and she wouldn't chance her heart again. She wasn't strong enough. It was going to hurt either way; better to do it now and try to move on with her life. Reese just wasn't sure what her life would look like without Dane in it. He had become her everything, she wasn't sure if she would want to exist in a world where she didn't get to see his face every day.

"You've been through so much, honey. I'm happy that you finally want to talk about everything," he said.

"What do you mean?" she questioned. Reese had a feeling that they weren't on the same page.

"You shot your own father, honey. You have to have mixed emotions about what you had to do—he was your dad." Reese almost wanted to laugh but from his expression, Dane was quite serious. He had no idea how easy a choice it was for her to shoot her father instead of losing him.

"I don't think you understand; I'd shoot that son-of-a-bitch all over again if it meant saving you, Dane," she admitted. "My father has never been a dad to me. He was always more concerned about his business. He didn't have time for me or my life and as a parent now, I see how wrong he was to treat me that way."

Dane nodded, "Yeah, I know I haven't been working this dad job long but I couldn't imagine not wanting to be a part of Cole's life." Hearing him say that gave her some piece of mind. If everything else fell apart between the two of them, Cole wouldn't lose his father. Her son would never know the sadness of being unwanted or unloved, as she had.

"I just don't know what I want, Dane. After everything just happened—you getting shot. I just don't know if I can let my heart be hurt. What would have happened to Cole and me if you would have died?" she asked. Dane stood and paced the floor in front of her.

"But I didn't die, I'm right here," Dane said, holding his arms wide open as if showing her he was alright. Reese couldn't erase the images of him lying in a pool of his own blood and thinking she had lost him for good. It hurt too much.

"You're a fireman, Dane. I know how dangerous your job is and I thought I could handle it. I told myself that you're good at your job and that you would be fine. But, seeing you in the hospital bed proved to me I was just fooling myself. You didn't die—this time, but what about the next? What happens when you run into a burning house and don't come back out?" Reese knew she was touching on a personal topic for Dane. He had told her how his father died saving a family. She was hitting below the belt but she wouldn't hold back now. He deserved her honesty—she owed him at least that much.

"That's not fair, Reese," Dane whispered. She hated seeing the pain that she was causing him but there was no other way to do this.

"I think I just need a few days to get my head on straight," Reese whispered. "Please understand," she said, reaching for Dane's arm. He pulled it out of her reach and his rejection felt like a slap. But she deserved it. She was telling the man she loved that she might not ever be ready to let him into her life or her heart.

Dane looked at her as if she lost her mind, and maybe she had. "You've been through a lot, honey. Why don't we slow things down and talk about this, rationally?" he asked. He seemed so hopeful that she'd agree to his reasoning and she was sure he had the patience of a saint, but she needed more than to just slow down. She needed some time to think about her next move.

"Please understand, Dane. I've spent my entire life doing what everyone else expected of me. I became a lawyer because it was what my parents expected of me. They wanted me to take over my father's business someday even when I told them that wasn't what I wanted."

"What exactly are you asking for, Reese? You expect me to just walk away from you? I love you," Dane growled. He sounded almost as if he was pleading with her and it just about gutted her. He deserved better but she wasn't sure she could give that to him.

Reese needed to figure out her own life. "I think I need to figure out myself before I can become a part of your life, Dane. Anything less wouldn't be fair to either of us."

"You're asking me to leave, aren't you?" Dane gasped.

"Yes," she whispered. "It's what is best for all of us."

"No, it's not what's fucking best for me, honey. You don't get to decide that." Dane's anger filled the space between the two of them and more than that, she could see his disappointment staring back at her in his beautiful green eyes. She felt physically pained by his hurt and she needed to end this because standing there having him look at her as if she betrayed him, was killing her.

"I don't know what else to say, Dane. It's just how I'm feeling," she mumbled.

"You know what, princess you take all the time you need. You know where to find me when you've made up your mind. I'll be in touch soon to work out seeing Cole. I won't lose him, Reese," Dane promised.

"No, of course, you won't. You are his father, Dane and I want him to have a relationship with you." Dane gave a curt nod and went back to their bedroom. Minutes felt like an eternity until he reappeared with his suitcase and jacket.

"I'll be at Toni's apartment for the night and then I'm heading home." His angry tone filled the room and she was sure she could feel it inside of her.

"Dane," she paused as he turned from leaving. Reese could see the hope in his eyes, that she was going to stop him from going but she wasn't. She wanted to, but Reese knew if she didn't take some time to sort through everything she had been through she might not come through the other side of the dark tunnel. "I'm sorry," she choked. "You will always be Cole's dad, even if we don't work out," she offered. He gave a curt nod and opened the front door.

"Well, at least you think I'm good enough for our son," he whispered and disappeared out of her apartment. Reese sobbed and collapsed onto her sofa. As if on cue, Cole started crying from his bedroom, having woken up from his nap yelling for his Daddy and it was all she could do not to yell for Dane to come back.

Dane

Two Weeks Later

Dane watched as Nico and Toni said their wedding vows and all he could think about was Reese. She was supposed to be his happily ever after, his future, his forever. Instead, he was alone while the woman he loved was making up her mind if she wanted those same things with him.

Since leaving New York two weeks ago, he had driven to the airport four times to catch a flight to go to her and Cole, only to talk himself out of it at the last minute. He had picked up his cell phone to call her a million times only to chicken out. He wanted to give Reese the time she asked for, but not being with her and Cole was killing him. If he had to spend another day without either of them, he felt like he was going to lose his shit.

A small reception followed the ceremony. It was set on the beach and it was absolutely perfect. But all Dane could think about was if he left at that moment, he could be to Reese and Cole by nightfall.

"Hey man," Jace said, stopping him from leaving the party. "You going so soon?" Dane looked over to where the happy couple was sharing their first dance and sighed.

"Yeah, I'm going to head to the airport," Dane admitted to his friend. Jace was Dane's former roommate and he probably knew him better than just about anyone else. Well—except Reese. Jace laughed, drawing Dane's attention back from where Nico and Toni were dancing.

"What's so fucking funny?" Dane grouched. Jace held up his hands as if in self-defense.

"Nothing, man. I've just lost count—how many trips to the airport will this be?" Dane shook his head. He hated Jace calling him on his shit again but he was right. He had been running back and forth to the airport and not taking a leap of faith to get on the fucking plane was just cowardice.

"I'm getting on the plane this time," Dane insisted. "I've given Reese two fucking weeks to figure her shit out and now I'm done waiting. She's being stubborn. I want her and I don't care about where we live or social statuses or any of that other shit. She and Cole are my whole life and I won't sit down here on this fucking island and wait for her to come to her senses." Jace's smile broadened and Dane felt a sudden need to punch his friend in the mouth.

"Woah there, big guy," Jace said as if noticing how angry Dane had become. "How about you just turn around and say all of that to your girl instead of doing something you'll regret." Dane was afraid to look behind himself for fear that Jace was having a joke at his expense. If Reese wasn't really standing there he didn't know if he'd be able to stand the disappointment. Dane slowly spun around to face Reese and she took his breath away.

"Hey," she whispered.

"Hey," he said back. Dane wasn't sure if he should pick her up and spin her around or sit down and brace himself for her to tell him that she didn't want to be with him anymore.

"Why are you here, Reese?" he asked, getting right to the point. He felt like his heart had already hoped for so much it would be wrong to want anything more—but he did. He wanted everything from Reese; he wanted her.

"Well, I was invited to the wedding," she sassed, looking back over her shoulder at the happy couple. "They look really happy together," she whispered. Reese seemed mesmerized by Nico and Toni swaying to the music and he cleared his throat, garnering her attention.

"Is that the only reason you are here, Reese?" His heart felt as though it was going to beat out of his damn chest when she turned back to face him, smiling up at him.

"Cole missed you. God, he wouldn't sleep for the first four days after you left. I think he needs to spend some time with you," she said. Dane knew spending time with Cole was more than he should have hoped for. Just weeks before, he didn't even know he had a son and now the toddler held a huge chunk of his heart. His son's mama held the other piece of it and Dane was scared to death she was about to break her part of it.

"Thanks for bringing him all the way down here, Reese. I'd love to spend some time with him," Dane all but whispered. He started for where Cole was playing in the sand because the alternative—standing there waiting for the woman he loved to tell him she wanted him—was tearing him in two.

"Um, Dane." Reese reached her hand out and touched his arm, stopping him from being able to take another step or another breath for that matter. She had the power to destroy his whole world and a part of him wanted to tell her to just give him a minute. If she was about to tell him good-bye, he was going to need a few minutes to get himself in check.

"What?" he questioned, refusing to look back down at her.

"I've missed you too," she whispered. "I've spent the last two weeks trying to figure out how we went from a one night stand to me feeling like one of my limbs was missing whenever you weren't in the same room with me. I felt like I was missing a piece of myself without you, Dane," she said. Reese removed her hand from his arm to cover her face. A sob escaped her chest and completely broke down his defenses. Dane pulled her into his arms.

"I've missed you too, baby—so much," he crooned. "Why did you take so long?" he asked.

"Well," she sniffled, "I've been told I'm quite stubborn." Dane threw back his head and laughed. It had been so long since he laughed, it felt pretty damn good.

"I'd say stubborn is an understatement, honey. Mules have nothing on you," he grumbled. She found the whole scene less funny.

"Well, from what I just heard from your conversation you went to the airport more than a few times and didn't follow through, so I guess we are both stubborn," she said.

Dane kissed the top of her head and pulled her snuggly against his body. "Fair point, honey. How about we both agree to work on that character flaw while we figure our way forward—together?" Reese hesitated for just a split moment and Dane could feel his damn breath hitch again.

"Yes, I'd like that." Reese nodded and smiled up at him. He didn't care who was watching, he picked her up and twirled her around like they had both lost their minds. "Cole and I would like to move here," she squealed. "In fact, I've been secretly working with Toni to come up with a little surprise for you," she whispered. Dane shot Toni a look and she sheepishly grinned and waved her fingers back at him.

"What kind of surprise?" he griped. "I really don't do surprises, honey."

Reese shrugged, "Well, you seemed to do just fine with my last surprise," she said motioning to Cole who was digging in the sand.

"Yeah well, he was a pretty damn awesome surprise," Dane agreed.

"I think you'll like this one too. Will you take a walk with me?" she asked.

"What about Cole?" Dane asked.

"I can watch him," Jace offered. Dane hadn't realized his friend was still listening in and from the smug smile on his face, Jace had heard their whole conversation.

"Thanks," Reese said. She handed over her bag of stuff Cole might need and grabbed Dane's hand, tugging him behind her.

"Want to tell me where you are dragging me off to, Princess?" he asked.

"I already did, Dane. It's a surprise," she loudly whispered.

They walked about four blocks down the beach and the closer they seemed to get to Reese's surprise, the more anxious she became. Her excitement was almost contagious and Dane found himself smiling at her breathy little giggles.

"Okay, close your eyes," she begged.

Dane looked around the area, knowing exactly where they were. He used to lifeguard this section of the beach and he was starting to think their two weeks apart had sent Reese over the edge. "Honey, I'm not sure that showing me the beach I know like the back of my hand qualifies as a surprise. I thought we were going to discuss our future and you and Cole moving down here but if you'd rather stay in New York, I'll move there. I've talked to my captain and he is willing to help me transfer to a company up there," Dane said. He shrugged as if it was no big deal, but honestly the thought of not living on the island made him a little sad. These past two weeks showed him living without Reese and Cole made him downright miserable. If she wanted to live on the moon, he'd find a way to pack his shit up and move there just to be with the two of them.

"Fine, don't close your eyes," she said. Her pout was pretty damn adorable and he couldn't help but steal a kiss from her. He'd been dying to get his lips on Reese's since he turned to find her standing behind him. She playfully swatted at his chest trying to push him away, which only made him want her more.

"Dane," she squealed. He smiled down at her and dipped his head for one more kiss. Reese covered her lips with her hand, blocking his path. "No," she said behind her hand. "I need to give you your surprise," she insisted but it sounded more like a muffled jumble of words. Dane knew his girl wasn't going to give up and the sooner she gave him his surprise, the sooner they could get back to kissing.

"Let's have it then," he said, giving into her was fun. Reese was always going to keep him on his toes and keep him guessing but he had to admit he liked the idea.

"Ta-da," she yelled, spreading her arms wide open, facing the sprawling beach house which sat back from the water just over the natural dunes. It had always been one of Dane's favorites with its multi-level decks and sun porch on the top; perfect for watching the small crafts come in from fishing all day or dolphin watching. But he couldn't figure out why Reese was so excited about the house.

"Um, yep. It's an awesome house," he said. Reese sighed as if exasperated by his lack of emotional response.

"Dane, it is an awesome house," she said. "And, it's our awesome house." Reese watched him and he knew he was totally fucking this all up. Until a few minutes ago, his future seemed dark and lonely. He wasn't sure if Reese would want a life with him and now, here she was shouting 'ta-da' at him and telling him they owned one of his favorite properties?

Reese giggled and framed his face with her slight hands. "It's not so bad, Dane. I bought us a house," she said.

"You bought us a house? This house?" He looked back at the sun-washed gray beauty and felt as though he was living in a dream.

"Yep, I sure did," she said. "When I called Toni to ask her to put me in touch with a realtor, she did one better and found me a few listings to fit my itinerary. She told me you always talked about this house and when I saw it was for sale, I scooped it up. I closed on it this morning just before heading over to the wedding. That's why I missed the ceremony."

"You're sure this is what you want, Reese? I meant what I said, I'll move to New York," Dane offered.

"I know that, Dane. I just don't see myself staying there," she admitted. "Especially since my heart is here with you. We made Cole here and I fell in love with you on this very island. I can't imagine a better place to live. Plus, I've been offered a pretty fantastic job working exclusively for Toni's company. I couldn't pass up the opportunity," she teased.

"Marry me," Dane said. "Be my wife." He sounded more like he was giving her a direct order then requesting her hand in marriage, but he didn't care. He wanted her and he wasn't about to wait another minute to make his future permanent with Reese.

This time Reese didn't hesitate, tears rolling down her soft cheeks, she nodded her agreement. "Yes," she choked, making him the happiest man on the planet.

"You've made me so happy, honey," he said. "Thank you," he whispered.

"I feel the same way about you, Dane. You have given me everything I've always wanted," she cried.

"Honey, you and Cole have become my whole life. You both are everything I never wanted and all I've ever needed." Dane picked Reese up in his arms and carried her towards their new home and their future together.

K.L. Ramsey

Reese

Six Months later

Reese watched as Dane played with Cole in the surf. The two had become inseparable and now there was going to be another baby—actually two babies—and she was thrilled, although she hoped her new husband was going to feel the same way. She discovered she was pregnant two days ago and she was waiting for just the right moment to tell him. Reese had an elaborate dinner planned for just the two of them tonight. Toni and Nico were taking Cole and she'd have Dane all to herself.

She decided to make them a nice picnic dinner and Nico offered to let them use his boat, although she knew close to nothing about boats; Dane was very capable when it came to all watercraft. He had been hinting he wanted to take her out on the water for months now since she and Cole moved to the island. Reese decided to surprise him tonight, giving him the perfect date and hopefully welcomed news about the newest additions to the family.

As soon as she got back to the island, Dane asked her to be his wife and she had to admit that a part of her worried everything was happening too fast. They had only been together for a short time and he asked her to spend forever with him. But, there was no way she was going to turn him down. Dane was her everything and now, he was her husband.

They had a small ceremony down by the water at sunset. It was followed by a reception on the beach in front of their new home and it was absolutely perfect. Her first failed attempt at throwing a wedding had cost hundreds of thousands of dollars and she ended up alone and miserable. Although, she thanked her lucky stars every day that she didn't end up married to David. His betrayal led her to go on her honeymoon alone and straight to Dane and she'd always be thankful for that. Dane had given her everything, Cole and a beautiful life together and now two more babies. Sometimes, Reese felt as though she was in a dream and honestly, she never wanted to wake up.

Instead of going on a honeymoon they stayed on the island moving both of their belongings into their new house. Dane's friends were quickly becoming her own and she loved that they all helped out and even took Cole to give them some privacy. They painted and decorated in between Dane convincing her to christen every room in the house with him—after all, it was their honeymoon and it was perfect.

Dane was standing by the back door, having returned from his walk down the beach with Cole and she could see his excitement over their date. She hadn't told him where they were going or what they were doing but her husband was always up for an adventure. "I dropped Cole off at Nico and Toni's. They said to tell you 'hi'," he said, picking up the wicker basket full of all of his favorite foods. "What did you pack in here? It's heavy," he said.

"Don't you dare look in that basket, Dane. It's a surprise and you'll ruin everything if you peek," she warned. She had packed a lot of food for just the two of them but she also put two little onesies and a sonogram picture she had done the day before. The doctor wanted to make sure she wasn't wrong about her due date because she was measuring a little larger than usual. She wasn't prepared for the news they were pregnant with twins but she left the doctor's office with the picture to prove it.

Dane held up his hands, as if in defense and smiled, "Alright, I'll be good and won't peek. Will you at least tell me where we are going?"

"Nope," she sassed. "You will just have to wait to see when we get there." Dane moaned and she giggled. Honestly, he was worse than Cole when it came to surprises.

She drove them both to the dock where Nico kept his boat and parked their SUV. "Here," she said, turning to hand him the keys to the boat. "We are borrowing Nico's boat for the night. Surprise!"

The look on Dane's face told her she had done a pretty good job at surprising him. "Wow honey, this is awesome," he said.

"I thought we could use a date night and well, Nico and Toni have agreed to keep Cole overnight and let us borrow the boat." Reese shrugged as if her scheming and planning wasn't a big deal.

"Well then, let's get this date night started," Dane said. He got out of their vehicle and rounded it to help her out, grabbing the picnic basket and overnight bag she snuck into the SUV. "You really have thought of everything," Dane wondered.

Reese just hoped he felt the same way when she explained to him he was going to be a father again, this time to twins.

K.L. Ramsey

Dane

Dane wasn't sure what had Reese so nervous, but he knew her well enough to know his wife had a few more surprises up her sleeve. He took them out onto calm water away from the island and any signs of life. It was just them, the sea, and the moon, and it was pretty damn near perfect.

"So, I um—well I packed a few of your favorite things for dinner and I hope you like everything." Reese's voice was almost a whisper as she handed him the wicker basket. He peeked into the basket and pulled out two baby outfits that were sitting on top of the food.

"They are cute, honey but I don't think they'll fit me," he joked. Reese rolled her eyes and reached into the basket to pull out a picture. He studied it and Reese was so quiet he could hear the water lapping at the side of the boat.

"I'm not sure what's happening here, honey. You seem nervous as hell and I'm starting to think you have something you want to share. Want to catch me up?" Dane was afraid to hope his hunch was correct but judging by the subtle hints Reese was dropping, she was either pregnant or was hoping to be soon. Either way, he was good. Dane loved Cole more than he thought possible and the idea of actually being there for both Reese and the new baby from the start this time, was something he dreamed of.

"Sorry, I was hoping to be better at this, but I guess I haven't had much experience in telling you that you are going to be a father," she whispered. "I mean, Cole was two when you found out so this is uncharted territory." Dane's heart felt as though it was going to beat out of his chest. Reese's fidgeting just about made him crazy. She was nervous about how he would take the news and that was the last thing he wanted.

"Come here, Reese," he said. She made her way across the deck and sat down next to him. "Are you saying we are going to have another baby?" he asked. Reese shyly nodded her head.

"Two babies actually," she murmured.

"Two babies?" he questioned. Reese nodded her answer again. Dane hooked his finger under her chin, lifting her face to look at him. "How long have you known?" he asked.

"Two days," she admitted. "I went to the doctor because I wasn't feeling well and he did a test just to rule out pregnancy. But, it came back positive so he did an exam and said I was measuring a little bigger than just a couple of months and then he did a sonogram," she rambled. "And well, we made twins."

Dane couldn't help his smile; he was so fucking happy but he worried Reese didn't feel the same way. She was nervous and he wondered if having twins wasn't exactly good news for her.

He pulled her onto his lap, wrapping his arms protectively around her body, feeling as though he was holding his whole world. "How do you feel about all of this?" he asked.

Reese sighed against him and snuggled into his hold. "I'm scared to death. They will outnumber us now and I'm not sure I'm ready for twins," she admitted. "I'm also worried you won't want them—want us." She ran her hand over her belly cupping her barely-there bump. Dane covered her hand with his own. Knowing his babies were inside of her did crazy things to his heart.

"I want them and God, I want you, Reese. You and Cole have become my entire world and now, you are giving me two new people to love. I'm so fucking happy, baby," he admitted. Dane pulled her in for a kiss and Reese wrapped her arms around his neck, turning to straddle his body.

"Is this okay?" he asked. "We can do this when you're pregnant?" Reese giggled and nodded. That was all of the confirmation he needed. He stood, lifting her with him to carry her below deck to the bedroom. Dane sat her on the edge of the bed and looked around the room. There were rose petals everywhere.

Dane looked down at Reese and cocked his eyebrow, as if in question. She shrugged, "I was hoping you'd be happy about our news," she said.

"How about you let me show you just how happy I am, honey," he said. Dane tugged her sundress over her head and hissed out his breath when he realized she was completely bare underneath. Reese smiled up at him and nearly took his breath away.

"I thought I'd make things easier on you," she said. Reese grabbed the hem of his t-shirt and yanked it over his head while he discarded his shorts. He wanted to waste no time getting inside of her and she seemed just as anxious as he felt.

"So fucking beautiful," he whispered, running his hands over her body. He laid Reese back against the bed and she pulled his body down with her. Dane spread her legs and sunk into her body, loving the breathy little moans and sighs that escaped her parted lips. She was so fucking sexy and all his. He pumped in and out of her body, taking what he needed from her and when she came it was his name she shouted out reminding him who she belonged to. Dane found his release and collapsed onto the bed next to her pulling her body in to fit against his own.

Reese was his—body, mind, and soul and he was so grateful she so freely gave herself to him. Dane wasn't sure what he had done to deserve her or the little family they were building but whatever it was, he wouldn't stop. They were his world.

"I love you," he whispered. Reese wrapped her arms around his waist.

"I love you too." Dane hauled her against his body knowing he would never find a more perfect woman to share his life with. Reese had become all he never wanted and everything he ever needed wrapped up in one sexy as sin package and he was the luckiest man on earth that she had given him a second chance.

The End

About K.L. Ramsey

Romance Rebel fighting for Happily Ever After!

K. L. Ramsey currently resides in West Virginia (Go Mountaineers!). In her spare time, she likes to read romance novels, go to WVU football games and attend book club (aka-drink wine) with girlfriends.

K. L. enjoys writing Contemporary Romance, Erotic Romance, and Sexy Ménage! She loves to write strong, capable women and bossy, hot as hell alphas, who fall ass over tea kettle for them. And of course, her stories always have a happy ending.

K.L. Ramsey's social media links

Facebook
https://www.facebook.com/kl.ramsey.58
(OR) https://www.facebook.com/k.l.ramseyauthor/
Twitter
https://twitter.com/KLRamsey5
Instagram
https://www.instagram.com/itsprivate2/
Pinterest
https://www.pinterest.com/klramsey6234/
Goodreads
https://www.goodreads.com/author/show/17733274.K_L_Ramsey
BookBub
https://www.bookbub.com/profile/k-l-ramsey
Amazon.com
https://www.amazon.com/K.L.-Ramsey/e/B0799P6JGJ/
Ramsey's Rebels
https://www.facebook.com/groups/ramseysrebels/
Website
https://klramsey.wixsite.com/mysite
KL Ramsey & BE Kelly's ARC Team-
https://www.facebook.com/groups/klramseyandbekellyarcteam
KL Ramsey & BE Kelly's Street Team
https://www.facebook.com/groups/klramseyandbekellystreetteam
Newsletter
https://mailchi.mp/4e73ed1b04b9/authorklramsey

BE Kelly's social media links

Facebook
https://www.facebook.com/be.kelly.564
Twitter
https://twitter.com/BEKelly9
Instagram
https://www.instagram.com/bekellyparanormalromanceauthor/
BookBub
https://www.bookbub.com/profile/be-kelly
Amazon
https://www.amazon.com/BE-Kelly/e/B081LLD38M
BE Kelly's Reader's group
https://www.facebook.com/groups/530529814459269/

More works by K.L. Ramsey

The Relinquished Series
Love Times Infinity
Love's Patient Journey
Love's Design
Love's Promise

Harvest Ridge Series
Worth the Wait
The Christmas Wedding
Line of Fire
Torn Devotion
Fighting for Justice

Last First Kiss Series
Theirs to Keep
Theirs to Love
Theirs to Have
Theirs to Take

Second Chance Summer Series
True North
The Wrong Mr. Right

Ties That Bind Series
Saving Valentine
Blurred Lines
Dirty Little Secrets

Taken Series
Double Bossed
Double Crossed

Owned
His Secret Submissive
His Reluctant Submissive

Alphas in Uniform
Hellfire

Coming Soon:
Royal Bastards MC
Savage Heat

Savage Hell MC Series
Roadkill

K.L. Ramsey

Works by BE Kelly (K.L.'s alter ego ...)

Reckoning MC Seer Series
Reaper
Tank
Raven

Perdition MC Shifter Series
Ringer

Printed in Great Britain
by Amazon